NORMAN McCOMBS

A REASON To BE

A Novel

GREENLEAF
BOOK GROUP PRESS

This is a work of fiction. Names, characters, businesses, organizations, places, events, and incidents are either a product of the author's imagination or are used fictitiously. Although most of the characters, organizations, and events portrayed in the novel are based on actual historical counterparts, the dialogue and thoughts of these characters are products of the author's imagination.

Published by Greenleaf Book Group Press
Austin, Texas
www.gbgpress.com

Distributed by Greenleaf Book Group

For ordering information or special discounts for bulk purchases, please contact Greenleaf Book Group at PO Box 91869, Austin, TX 78709, 512.891.6100.

Design and composition by Greenleaf Book Group
Cover design by Greenleaf Book Group
Cover Images: ©iStockphoto/detshana and ©Shutterstock/margit777

Publisher's Cataloging-in-Publication data is available.

Print ISBN: 978-1-62634-733-5

eBook ISBN: 978-1-62634-734-2

Part of the Tree Neutral® program, which offsets the number of trees consumed in the production and printing of this book by taking proactive steps, such as planting trees in direct proportion to the number of trees used: www.treeneutral.com

TreeNeutral

Printed in the United States of America on acid-free paper

20 21 22 23 24 25   10 9 8 7 6 5 4 3 2 1

First Edition

Dedicated to Grace Nancy Seitz-McCombs.
My love. My life. My inspiration.

100% of author royalties donated to
the Alzheimer's Association.

McCombs Family Tree

Big Thomas Mackintosh (Tomaidh Mòr)
circa 15th century
Glen Shee, Scottish Highlands

John Gordon Macomb + Jane Macomb
b. 1717 in Ballyclare, County Antrim, Ireland*
d. 1796 in New York, United States

Alexander Macomb +
Mary Catherine Macomb (Navarre)
b. 1748 in County Antrim, Ireland
d. 1831 in Washington, D.C., United States

Timothy McCombs + Sarah McCombs
b. 1765 in Ireland
d. Unknown

John McCombs + Magdalene McCombs
b. 1792 in VT, United States
d. 1865 in St. Catharines, Ontario, Canada

Major General Alexander Macomb, Jr.
b. 1782 in Detroit, MI, United States
d. 1841 in Washington, D.C., United States

Rev. Jacob McCombs
b. 1825 in Dunnville, Ontario, Canada
d. 1911 in Dunnville, Ontario, Canada

Norman Archibald McCombs + Edna Sephronia Farr
b. 1851 in St. Catharines, Ontario, Canada
d. 1938 in Haldimand Co., Ontario, Canada

Robert "Bobby" McCombs + Gladys McCombs
b. 1892 in Ontario, Canada
d. 1967 in Buffalo, NY, United States

*All dates and locations shown correspond
to male members of the McCombs family.

Douglas McCombs

Prologue

*"Clansmen believed that courage
flowed down the generations."*
—**Alistair Moffatt**, *The Highland Clans*

"We will get caught," young Thomas whispered to his little brother, who was lying prostrate beside him in the heather. "And Da will kill us both."

"Don't be so afraid of your own shadow! No one can see us up here," Douglas whispered back. He was the younger of the two brothers, that was true, but Douglas was also braver, able to marshal his courage even when Thomas's faltered. Douglas tucked a long black wisp of hair behind his ear. "Now hush or we *will* get caught."

The tartans they wore were spread out over the heather, the boys' white shirts hanging loosely from their sinewy frames. They were not dressed appropriately for the secrecy of their outing—the colors of their tartans were bright and new and would be easily spotted by anyone who stood amid the knee-high purple heather.

The night before, their father—Big Thomas as he was known throughout Glenshee—had fanned the tartans out ceremoniously as he presented them to the boys. He, too, had been wearing the same bright blue and green plaid. The colors of these new tartans confused the boys at first. For as long as they could remember, their father had donned the red and green colors of the Mackintosh clan. In fact, everyone who belonged to the Chattan clans surrounding them had worn the colors of Mackintosh.

"Yer mam's done a beautiful job, boys," he said. Big Thomas handed a blue-and-green tartan to each of his sons, asking them to remove their old tartans as he did so. "Wear them with pride. Now undress and give me your old ones."

To the boys' astonishment and delight, they stood naked and watched as their father took their old tartans and threw them into a raging fire. Apprehensive, the brothers looked back at their mother for guidance. When she nodded her approval, they whooped and danced naked around the fire as their father laughed with pride.

"From this day forward, boys, we no longer answer to Chief Mackintosh," Big Thomas declared, the sound of his voice loud and clear in the night air. "No sons of mine will answer to or pay a man they have never seen, who has *never stepped foot* in these glens—yet requires that we pay him for the land we live on! We will show no loyalty to that which does not deserve to be honored."

The boys nodded solemnly to show their understanding. As Big Thomas continued speaking, the brothers hastened to put on their new tartans. The story their father told was one they had heard many times, one that had been recounted at bedtime and again any time the boys' character or courage was in question.

"We are descended from a great line of men. From William, the seventh Chief of Mackintosh, the eighth of the Clan Chattan, who reigned during the great Scottish King David II. His sons Adam and Sorald were the rightful heirs of this chiefdom—though they could never be acknowledged, as they were born bastards. A shame! A waste!

"Adam was the largest, bravest, and *most feared* man in the chiefdom. Big Adam, your great-great grandfather, was rightful chief of the clan. Big Adam, the father of my grandfather, Big Thomas—it was he who fought off our enemies and protected this land and all of our progeny. It was *Adam*, not some Mackintosh chief, who defended our land from marauders and the evil southerners who wished to 'civilize' us. It was *he* who fought bravely alongside William Wallace to keep Scotland free.

"I am Big Thomas, son of Thomas, son of Big Thomas, son of Adam, son of William. We are now and always have been *MacThomas*."

The boys knew this tale by heart and could repeat it word for word. But this time, the boys listened raptly. Something was brewing: They were wearing these new colors now, and there were rumors of a battle of Glenshee, a showing of strength between the two clans. The winner would take the land, the children, and most horrifying of all—their mother. Big Thomas had already declared that no other man would raise his children, mind his land, or lay with his wife. He would fight to the death before he ever let that happen. For Big Thomas, death was preferable to a life without his Eve and his two boys, Thomas and brave little Douglas.

Now, watching from their hiding spot amid the heather on the high hill, the boys watched as Big Thomas stepped out into the glen. He stood with the entire Thomas clan, all descendants of the bastards of William, arranged in battle order. Clustered in groups by family, each generation stood behind the last—fathers in front of their sons, brother beside brother, and all of the elder men making up the front line.

The oldest, wisest, and most experienced warriors were always in the front during battles. The Scots had long understood that courage flowed down through generations, that it sprang forth as a tiny drop from a single ancestor and grew over time, eventually accumulating en masse within each man as the generations proceeded. They believed that the youngest warriors—those who stood in the back of the line—had the courage of one hundred generations pumping through their veins. They stood in the back, away from the front line of battle, as it would be with them that the destiny of all would be entrusted.

The boys held their breath, watching as their father, Big Thomas, a massive man in his own right, took his axe in his left hand and drew his broadsword high above his head with his right. Once the blade was aloft and all eyes focused on him, Big Thomas recited all two hundred years of his lineage back to their ancestor William, born in the year 1300. In these days, all warriors did such a thing. When their father told them tales around the fire, the boys loved to hear stories of how such battles began—fearless warriors raising their swords above their heads and regaling the enemy with their fearsome lineage. The brothers settled in. They knew this would take a long time.

True to their father's tales, every single man in the front line of his father's clan drew their swords and proudly shouted the same lineage. Once they were finished, it was time for the enemy to do the same. On the other side of the glen, the Mackintosh clan leader drew his sword and raised it aloft to begin the recitation of his lineage. But before his voice could break the tension that hung thick in the air, Big Thomas charged across the field, leaving all his kin behind him, their swords drawn above their heads. As Thomas ran, he took aim with his double-bladed Lochaber axe at the Mackintosh clan leader—the man who, only a day before, had come to his door to claim his wife. With strength and deftness unlike anything the boys had seen before, their father hurled the axe at the man who would strip him of his family.

The boys shot to their feet as they watched the axe fly across the field, blade over handle, before burying itself in the Mackintosh leader's skull—cleaving him right between the eyes. The brothers watched in horror as the man's lifeblood flowed from the grievous wound and the Mackintosh leader fell back into the heather, dead.

Shocked by the violence that for the first time wasn't safely contained in a bedtime story told around the fire, the boys turned to run for their lives, away down the glen. But just then, a roar rose up from the field of battle behind them. The two clans were descending on each other, the two lines of men smashing headlong into one another. The boys couldn't help but turn and watch to see if their father, their uncles, and their older cousins would survive. Neither one wanted to see their mother ripped from their home if their father died. Neither one wanted to wear any tartan other than the one their father had given them the night before.

The two boys knelt in the grass and watched the chaos below. Axes flew through the air, sinking into chests with a sickening sound. Those who threw the axes chased down their targets, ripping their weapons violently from the bodies so they could throw them yet again. Some men fought with short swords, plunging the blades into their enemies' bellies. Others wielded their broadswords, oftentimes decapitating their enemies in a single blow. Still others aimed crossbows with such precision they didn't have to step forward from the line to slay their targets across the broad field.

By the time the sun had fully risen that morning, Mackintosh men lay scattered across the glen—their blank eyes open skyward, their bodies torn and broken, their red tartans made redder with gore. But there were blue tartans spread out in the fields as well. During the onslaught, the boys had lost sight of their father. Now with great trepidation, they struggled to see who remained standing.

As they searched for their father's face among the bloodied survivors, they heard footsteps approach from behind, crunching through the heather.

Frightened, the brothers cowered. A man stepped forward, tall, broad, and filthy, his tartan so matted with gore its color was unintelligible. Fear gripped the boys tightly, and neither one seemed to draw breath for a long moment as they stared at the bloody stranger.

"What are two Mac-om boys doin' in the heather like scared li'l Mackintoshes?" came the stranger's booming voice, familiar to them both. "You'll rise up, you will! You'll stand like men of honor! We Mac-oms are descended from the great Thomas, and you descend from a great Thomas too. You and your line and all the men in it from now until judgment day will have the courage and honor to defend your women to the death. You will never, ever hide amid the heather again. Do ya hear me?"

"Yes, Da," the boys, stricken, replied as one.

"Now what's your name, boy?"

"Thomas, son of Thomas," the boy said proudly. "I am a MacThomas!" He raised his arm as if holding a broadsword and heading into battle.

"And you, boy," Big Thomas said to his younger son. "What's *your* name? Where do you come from?"

"I am Douglas, son of Thomas, son of Thomas, son of Big Thomas. Son of Adam. I am *Mac-om*," Douglas said, repeating his father's abbreviation of *MacThomas*. "And like me father, like all the great warriors before me, I am a warrior!"

"Yes, yes you are."

Big Thomas leaned over and grabbed the two boys, drawing them to him in an embrace tighter than either brother could recall receiving from his father before that moment or afterward. Pulling away from the boys with a touch of reluctance that neither one noticed, Big Thomas bent down and picked up young Douglas, swinging him up on his shoulders.

The three walked down the hill together, through the heather and back home to Eve, who had kept the fire burning in their hearth all this harrowing day long. A serene and loving smile spread across Eve's face when she caught sight of her boys returning from the fray. Though as a mother she did not defend her family by the sword, she had spent the day busily distracting herself from the battle she could hear raging outside by preparing an elaborate feast, keeping faith that the angels would protect her husband from harm, guide his hand to victory in battle, and bring him and her boys home for supper.

1

WAS SHE EVER REALLY THERE?

*A*s a sunbeam broke through the crack in the floor-length windows of his Fifth Avenue brownstone, falling in a long, bright line across his bed, Douglas McCombs turned away and pulled the comforter up over his head. He was in no mood for such a glaring display of optimism. The nerve of the sun, daring to rise on yet another day.

This dusty shaft of sunlight was only the first of many provocations to greet him. Across the room, in the pocket of his jacket, which was draped over several days' accumulation of dirty laundry, his phone vibrated incessantly. He had lost count of how many calls had come in, but he estimated this latest one was the fifth or sixth of the morning. Douglas had no intention of answering the phone, let alone getting up and crossing the room to turn it off. Any movement, even the slightest, was too exhausting to even think about.

Besides, he knew who was trying to call him. It was his friend Mark. The younger man was like a son to Douglas, and he was the only one who called these days. If it were Mark, then he could wait. In fact, everyone could wait. That's all that was left to do with his life anyway, Douglas thought. Wait. Wait for it to all be over. Wait for the pain—that dull, incessant ache that permeated everything—to disappear and take any vestige of himself that still remained along with it.

True, Douglas's entire body ached, but his heart ached most of all. It felt a lot like it had in high school, when he'd recovered and then landed on a fumbled football moments before a pile of players jumped on him. His heart had felt the impact first back then. As the mass of other players piled on and crushed him, it took all the energy Douglas had to just breathe.

But the pain he felt now wasn't like that moment in high school. When the other players had clambered off him, he could breathe again. But Douglas couldn't find relief now. His heart ached relentlessly, and there was no escape. He had felt this way for *months*. He could pinpoint the precise moment when he felt his heart break. It was when the EMTs had come bounding up the stairs of the home he had shared with Hope for nearly fifty years. The EMTs had wheeled the gurney up beside Douglas's marriage bed and pulled the sheets back to reveal Hope's small, wasted, and impossibly fragile body. Seeing Hope so exposed, Douglas felt as though someone had punched him in the chest. All the air had escaped him and he couldn't catch his breath.

How did this happen? he had thought. *Where did my Hope go?*

This moment was the first time Douglas had really seen her the way that other people had. He could still remember the look on the EMT's face, looking first down at Hope and then back to Douglas.

"How long has she been like this?" the other EMT asked, checking Hope's vitals.

Douglas had been confused by the question. Were they asking how long had she been in *bed*? Douglas wasn't entirely sure at the moment. Weeks? Months? Either answer seemed plausible to him in that moment. Did they mean how long had she been *catatonic*? Unresponsive? Not herself? Douglas didn't know how to answer. He couldn't tell them how long Hope had suffered from Alzheimer's. He just looked back at the EMTs, baffled and confused.

"Have you been taking care of her all by yourself, sir?" the second EMT asked, more kindly this time.

"Yes," Douglas said. At least he seemed to be able to answer that.

"For how long?"

"About, I don't know, the past five years or so," Douglas said. He pushed his hand over his matted hair and looked around the room. He saw it, too, as if for the first time, now that he found there were strangers in his bedroom. Hope's adult diapers were stacked on the dresser. Empty and half-full prescription bottles were clustered on the bedside table. Dirty sheets and towels were piled high in one corner. *What a mess*, Douglas thought, suddenly self-conscious.

"Sir? You've been caring for your wife *all by yourself* for five years?" the EMT asked, shock in his voice.

Douglas nodded.

It was true. For five years, he had taken care of Hope. At first, taking care of her meant covering up for her. Whenever she forgot an appointment, a beloved cousin's name, or an item from the grocery store, Douglas would handle it. As time went on, his role became more obvious. He would tell her something he did or something someone had said, and a few minutes later she would ask about the very same thing. Realizing she had forgotten something, she would get upset. Seeing Hope agitated upset Douglas too, so he did whatever he could so she wouldn't get too flustered. He would simply repeat the story again and again. Douglas also took great care to make sure none of his associates knew about what was happening with Hope. He *never* mentioned it. He couldn't even really say why he had felt the need to keep her condition so secret. After all, he was an inventor and a designer of state-of-the-art, life-saving health-care equipment. He was a celebrated biomedical engineer. Everyone would understand.

If he were being honest, Douglas would admit that he didn't *want* them to understand. He wanted his *wife* back. More than anything, he was overwhelmed by a fierce desire to protect her. She had always been a stunning beauty—bright and witty, too. He didn't want anyone to pity her or to upset her in any way. As her condition worsened, keeping her calm and happy was no easy task. Hope often became so moody that she wasn't herself. Keeping her gradual deterioration a secret became increasingly difficult. Douglas began mostly keeping her at home. As the disease progressed, she forgot how to dress herself, brush her hair, or find her way to the bathroom. Eventually, he had to bathe her and take her to the bathroom himself. He even had to feed her, holding the spoon up to her speechless lips, encouraging her to chew or swallow, whatever was required. She couldn't seem to remember how to do those things either. As the years went on, Douglas began spending his nights awake, sitting beside her and attending to her every need. She needed around-the-clock care.

Somewhere in all that caregiving, Douglas had forgotten that he needed care too. By the time he called the EMTs for help, he couldn't remember the last time he had showered, eaten, or had a decent night's unbroken sleep. He felt an overwhelming thirst, and he couldn't even remember the last time he had drunk a glass of water.

"Sir, is there anyone you can call? Is there anyone who can help *you* now?" the EMT asked. He and his partner began gingerly wheeling the gurney out of the bedroom, Hope lying on it, helpless and still.

"I don't know. I guess I could call my friend Mark," Douglas said absently. "He's like family."

"Call him. Call him right now," the EMT said gently. "You're going to need someone to help you through this."

Douglas nodded. His gaze drifted down to the gurney again, and he stepped forward to stand beside it. He reached out to take Hope's hand.

"You'll take good care of her? You'll be sure to—" Douglas stopped himself. There was nothing more that he or anyone could do.

"Yes, sir," the EMT said. He patted Douglas's hand warmly. "We'll take it from here, but I really want to make sure you're all right. Please go call someone."

"I will," Douglas promised, choking the words out between quiet sobs.

Douglas hadn't yet realized that Hope would never return to their home. Just as, in the early days of her disease, he hadn't realized that *she* would never return to her old self again. The Hope he knew, loved, and adored his entire life had never come back to him. It had made him wonder: Had she ever really been there?

Douglas had loved Hope since he first laid eyes on her. They were just teenagers then, and she had another beau at the time. But a boyfriend had hardly been a deterrent to Douglas. He remembered the day he saw her for the first time. He could close his eyes and replay the memory over and over again in his mind's eye as if no time had passed. When he did so, it always felt like the precise moment Hope turned around and looked at him for the very first time. It was as if the entire world had melted away, and there, floating above it all, was Hope—beautiful, slender, delicate, vivacious. With her shining green eyes and a wide-open smile, she had captivated him fully. She was just a girl back then, sure, but still he had been sure she was the only woman for him.

Theirs was a love affair for the ages—or so everyone told him. Everyone, including Douglas himself, seemed to take it for granted that he and Hope would be together for many years to come. He was only sixty-five and in the prime of his career when Hope started to slip into oblivion. She had always been so young and vibrant. *How could so much change so quickly? How could everything they had together have simply slipped away into the ether?*

These were the questions that kept Douglas up at night now when he lay awake in his new home—the home he refused to leave. It was a different home than the one he and Hope had created together. Douglas had left that home the day Hope had, and he had not returned. But he couldn't bring himself to sell the house, either, so he had turned over the property and its care to his nephews. Douglas couldn't be bothered with the caretaking of a home. He much preferred lying in bed all day and sleeping to facing a day without Hope. There was nowhere he had to be. Nothing pressing he had to do. For years he had operated his business over the phone so he could care for Hope full time.

And he could afford to do it. He had more money than he would ever be able to spend in a lifetime. Some would say Douglas was an accomplished man, with hundreds of patents and inventions to his credit. In fact, only a few years before, he had found himself at the White House in front of the president himself, receiving the National Medal of Technology and Innovation for his inventions and advances in health science technology.

Before Hope's diagnosis, they had planned to enjoy their success by continuing to travel the world. They would visit their homes in Tuscany, Vienna, and Switzerland. They would dine in fine restaurants. He would keep working on researching the genealogy of his Scottish-American heritage.

All that seemed silly now. Ridiculous, even. *What was the point of traveling? What was the point of money and accolades without Hope? Who cared about ancient ancestry without a meaningful legacy? What did any of it matter?* He and Hope had no children. His siblings were all deceased. *What then, if anything, does a man have to live for without the love of his wife? Without children? Without something productive to do? What was the point of it all? Why even love anything to begin with, if it's going to be ripped away eventually?*

Douglas was hopeless. He was, to his mind, the end of the line. He was the last surviving member of his family. He had no progeny to carry his name into the future and, for all he knew, no past. His family never talked about where they had come from or what their ancestors had done. Douglas had spent most of his adult life deeply ashamed of where he came from. It was too much for him to even talk about sometimes. Before Hope, there hadn't been much to life. Now, after having lost Hope, Douglas realized there wasn't much after her either.

Eventually, the phone stopped vibrating in his jacket pocket. He was relieved at the silence. But within minutes, a loud, obnoxious pounding at the front door had replaced the annoying, but at least relatively quiet, buzzing sound of the phone.

"Dammit," Douglas said. "Go away!"

Of course Douglas realized no one could hear him, seeing as he was almost two stories up from the front door, which was at street level.

"Douglas! Douglas!" he heard someone shouting from the street below. "Are you in there? Are you okay?"

It was Mark; Douglas recognized his voice.

Slowly pushing the covers off of himself, Douglas groaned, and he made his way out of the bed and across the room to grab a robe.

"I'm coming! I'm coming!" Douglas shouted back. He headed down the stairs toward the door and opened it.

"Jesus Christ, Douglas! I thought you were . . ." Mark left the thought unfinished.

"Dead?" Douglas said matter-of-factly. "Might as well be." He turned away and started walking back up the stairs. He didn't bother to invite Mark in, knowing the younger man would march right into the house anyway.

"Hey, get back down here!" Mark called after him. "We need to talk!"

Douglas turned on the stairs and regarded Mark for a moment. He looked like an angel, framed by the light pouring in behind him through the open door. Mark was dashing and impeccably dressed—his suit perfectly tailored, his shirt starched, his hair combed and wet. Mark's expression was filled with youth, hope, and promise.

It all irritated the hell out of Douglas.

"I don't want to talk. I don't want to do anything. I'm going back to bed."

"No you're not!" Mark insisted. "It's almost ten o'clock on a Tuesday, Douglas. There's a whole life out there waiting to be lived. Now what you're going to do is shower, shave, and then we're going out for a hot meal. Let's go."

"No!" Douglas refused, his voice sounding more petulant than he would have liked.

"Yes!" Mark replied, not missing a beat. "I am *not* arguing with you. I took the day off of work and came up here to make sure you weren't dead. It's the least you can do for me. I was worried sick." Mark closed the door behind him pointedly, as if emphasizing his statement.

"You expect me to *feel bad* for you?" Douglas asked. "I didn't ask you to come here. I don't need anyone's help. What's it to you, anyway?" He had progressed from petulant child to rebellious teen in less than thirty seconds.

"What's it to me? *What's it to me?*" Mark asked, taken aback. "I'm worried about you, Douglas! You promised me that if we moved you here, you would be better. You said you didn't want to be in that old house with all those things that reminded you of

Hope. You said that would help you. You've been here for *months* and you haven't done a thing," Mark said. He was making his way down the foyer, peering into first the living and dining rooms and then the kitchen, where boxes remained shoved up against walls. "You haven't *unpacked*," Mark said, stepping into the kitchen. He walked up to the refrigerator and pulled it open. "You haven't gone grocery shopping."

"I order out. You can do that in Manhattan, you know," Douglas said dryly, sinking into a chair at the kitchen table. "I never have to leave here if I don't want to. And I *don't* want to."

"Then what do you do all day, Douglas?"

"Mostly, you're looking at it," Douglas said, shrugging.

"You mean to tell me that you walk around in your robe and lie in bed all day?" Mark asked.

"Well, I don't always wear my robe," Douglas quipped.

"Douglas, come on, this is serious!" Mark said. "You're obviously, I don't know, *depressed*. You don't have to live this way, Douglas. This is no way to live."

"Who says?" Douglas asked, crossing his arms. "Who says it's no way to live? I like it just fine."

"Really?" Mark asked, skeptical. "You *like* living alone? You *like* not being productive? You *like* lying around in bed all day? Come on! Who are you fooling? You used to build life-saving machines, for God's sake! You used to travel the world. You used to eat in the finest restaurants. You've dined with *the president*, for crying out loud!"

"The operative words are *used to*, Mark. Those days are long gone," Douglas said. "There's nothing here for me now. I just have to bide my time."

"Until what?" Mark asked. "What are you waiting for?"

"Waiting for God," Douglas said.

Mark paused and thought for a moment, gazing at Douglas, wistful. "This isn't you talking, Douglas."

"Who else do think is talking to you here?" Douglas said, gesturing around the empty kitchen.

"No, what I mean is, this isn't the Douglas *I know*," Mark said. "The Douglas I know cared about how he looked. Was vibrant, healthy. He showered, shaved, and took care of himself, if you can imagine. And he took care of others, too. The Douglas I know was *excited* about life. Why, just a few years ago, you were standing on the White House lawn. Do you remember that moment? Do you remember what you said to me?"

"No," Douglas said quietly, and, for a moment, he seemed interested in what Mark had to say. Mark sensed it and seized the opportunity.

"Yes, you do remember. You absolutely do. Come on. *What did you say?*"

There was a beat of silence as Douglas searched his memory of that day. He found the moment and gingerly peered into it, falling more deeply into the memory as the details came back to him.

"I said, '*How did I get here?*'" Douglas answered. "That's what it was—what I said. I was standing at the entrance of the East Wing. I had just passed through three levels of security and was all alone for a moment. I stopped and just stood there, thinking, *How in the world did I get here?*"

"And what did that make you want to do?" Mark asked, now bending down in front of his friend so that he was staring Douglas right in the eyes.

"I wanted to find out how I got there," Douglas said. "I wanted to figure out how a poor little kid like me ended up at the White House. I wanted to know where I came from. I wondered, *How did I get here? Was it Hope? Was it my upbringing? Or did it go back*

*even further—to the Highlands of Scotland where my ancestors sup-
posedly came from?"*

"And don't you still want to know?" Mark asked. "Where did
that desire go, Douglas?"

"I don't know. I guess I don't see the point in any of it anymore.
Doesn't seem to make much sense to get excited about anything—
anything at all, really—if it's all going to end eventually."

"What if you just *try*, Douglas? Just, I don't know, try to do
something—anything?"

"I don't want to, Mark. I don't want to live," Douglas said flatly.
"Don't you see? There's really no point to it, not without her."

"Now we both know that's not true," Mark said. He had stood
up and was visibly annoyed. "You've been putting her on a pedes-
tal for years, and it's high time . . ."

"Shut up, Mark! Don't you say *one bad thing* about Hope! Don't
you dare!"

Mark pinched his lips into a thin, white line and shook his head.
"I'm sorry, Douglas, I didn't mean to upset you. It's just that . . ."

"Don't say another word, Mark, not about my Hope,"
Douglas warned. "You know how I feel about that. It's all in
the past now . . ."

"Exactly, Douglas, *it's in the past*. And you're still here. You're
still very much alive and healthy—in fact, you have a few decades
left in you," Mark said. "You can't spend decades up in that bed.
You have to live your life. You have to get out there and do what
you have always wanted to do. Why don't we start small—let's
say a shower, a shave, and a walk? Please? Do it for me? I am not
asking you to get over Hope. I am not asking you to do anything
else but leave the house for a little while."

Douglas, leveraging himself against the table, forced himself
up. "Just this once. Then you'll leave me alone."

"Sure, Douglas. You just have to shower and go for a walk once, and then I'll leave you alone," Mark agreed. "I'll wait down here. Now go get moving."

• • •

It was past noon by the time Douglas and Mark finally left the house and made their way down Fifth Avenue.

"Let's cut through the park," Mark advised. "No sense walking on these crowded sidewalks. Let's take our time re-introducing you to humanity, shall we?"

"Whatever you want. It's your walk," Douglas said dismissively.

"It's *our* walk," Mark corrected him. "And let's make it a standing date at noon each day. I'll come on my lunch hour. Come on, it'll be fun! Look at the vibrant orange on these trees! I think fall is the best time of the year in New York. Don't you?"

"Well, it doesn't smell like garbage and piss anymore, so that's an improvement," Douglas offered.

"Look at you, Douglas, looking on the bright side already," Mark said, elbowing him.

"Take it easy, Mark."

"Say, listen, Douglas, while we're out," Mark began coolly, "why don't we, I don't know, head up to the library or something? We could check out a book or two about the Scottish Highlanders, or something about the McCombs family tree. Didn't you tell me you descended from some pretty famous Americans? Anyone worth naming?"

"I see what you're doing, Mark," Douglas replied immediately. "I won't take the bait. You're just trying to get me excited about genealogy again."

"See?" Mark said and smiled. "You're too smart to be sitting around at home doing nothing. Come on, let's just start with something. Anything. All I am asking is for you to read a book.

Talk to someone. So you have to have a reason to get up in the morning. We all need a reason to get up in the morning."

"Yeah? Is that so?" Douglas asked. "Well, my reason isn't here anymore. So I guess I'm done for."

"Well, it may be true that your reason isn't here anymore, Douglas. But you can find a *new* reason. It's our job to find a reason—a purpose. It's not always there right in front of us. It's not always so obvious. You have to *create* it," Mark said, the passion in his voice rising until Douglas felt stunned into silence.

"I suppose," Douglas agreed quietly.

• • •

For the next few days, however grudgingly, Douglas did exactly as Mark instructed. He set his alarm every night, and when he awoke each morning, he forced himself out of bed and took a shower. He shaved, made his bed, and did not get back into it until it was time to sleep in the late evening. He unpacked all the boxes. He hung his clothes in the closet. He went to the grocery store and bought a single-cup coffeemaker, pods, and juice. Each task gave way to a new one, and before he knew it, momentum had taken over. After awhile, Douglas found it impossible to sit still for long at all. With each new day and each new activity introduced, Douglas found he had more energy. The more he moved, the less he thought, and the less he thought, the less plagued by haunting memories he felt.

Within a month, Douglas had established a consistent routine, which included taking a midday constitutional through the park with Mark at noon. After his morning chores were done, he left the brownstone, crossed Fifth Avenue, said hello to Mark, and the two entered Central Park together. They took the same route each day. After parting ways with Mark, Douglas would walk to a nearby coffee shop, order a cappuccino, and read the newspaper until it was time to go and pick up dinner.

For reasons unbeknownst to him, one day Douglas surprised himself, and when they had reached the south end of Central Park, he looked up at The Plaza Hotel. For the first time, he suggested to Mark that they break their routine.

"What do you say we leave the park today?" Douglas said, looking out across the street.

"Why, that would be great, Douglas!" Mark replied supportively. "Want to walk with me back down to my office?"

"Let's do it. I feel up for it." Douglas nodded.

"Terrific," Mark said with a smile, but trying not to make too much of a fuss.

As the two friends walked down Fifth Avenue and neared 42nd Street, they came upon the iconic lion statues standing guard outside the New York Public Library. A smile crept across Mark's face.

"Hey, on second thought, why don't you go on in here, and I'll head down to work by myself?" Mark said, gesturing nonchalantly toward the library.

"I don't think so," Douglas said, shaking his head firmly.

"Come on, go on in and talk to a librarian. They can look up books on the computer and grab one for you. You don't have to do any of the work. It's a small step," Mark said, pulling Douglas by the hand up the steps.

"Come on, Mark. I just want to walk. Let's go," Douglas protested. He refused to look at the library as he tried to pull his hand away.

"You don't have to do it all today. Just start small," Mark encouraged him.

"Dammit, Mark. Can't you leave well enough alone?" Douglas asked, abruptly pulling away while turning around. In one swift motion, he broke free from Mark and inadvertently bumped into a brightly dressed woman who had been passing by them on the stairs at that exact moment. Douglas, not unaware of his large stature, felt the power of the impact as he knocked into her, causing her to drop her bag and the book she was carrying.

"Oh my gosh, I'm so sorry! I didn't see you there!" Douglas said. He immediately bent over and attempted to help the woman gather the belongings that had fallen out of her bag.

"I'm fine, I'm fine," she reassured him. "I don't need any help." She kneeled down to pick up her things, adjusting her fuchsia and lime green scarf as it blew in the breeze.

Douglas bent down to help her and found himself staring at this arresting stranger. He was struck by the shape and depth of her dark brown eyes. To him, she looked the way he imagined an Egyptian goddess must.

"What?" she asked, sensing that he was staring at her.

"You have beautiful eyes," Douglas said, much to his own shock.

"Oh, thank you," she said politely, if absently, collecting tubes of lipstick and packets of Kleenex and putting them back in her bag.

"I didn't mean to frighten you," Douglas said. He rose to his feet and extended a hand to help her up from the ground.

Reluctantly, she reached out and accepted his hand.

When Douglas took her hand in his, a warm feeling washed over him—one that he couldn't explain or describe. He blushed.

Mark noticed that Douglas seemed flustered and jumped in.

"So sorry about that," he told the woman kindly. "We were talking and got distracted. My name is Mark Collier, and this is my friend Douglas McCombs. We were just heading into the library too. Is there anything we can do for you to make it up? Buy you a coffee?" Mark laughed nervously.

"I'm fine, thank you. It didn't look like you were going in. It looked like you were turning around and leaving. It's okay. It doesn't matter. I'm running late. I have to get back to work; my lunch break is over." With that, she started briskly up the stairs.

"Wait. You work here?" Douglas called after her.

The woman hesitated and turned slightly to look at him. Douglas could tell she didn't want to disclose where she worked. Such information could be sensitive, of course. She lived in New York after all. It wasn't common practice to tell strangers where you worked, and for good reason.

"I really have to go," the woman said politely.

"What's your name?" Douglas asked before she could turn to go. "I'd really like to make it up to you. I am truly sorry."

"It's Susannah," the woman offered. "Most people call me Suzy. And you don't have to make anything up to me. I am fine." With that, she turned abruptly and hustled up the stairs.

"Okay! I understand!" Douglas called after her again. "I'll see you around. I come here quite often."

Mark shot him a smirk, which Douglas returned with a withering look of his own—as if to say, *Not one word out of you.*

Douglas watched in awe as the energetic woman bounded up the steps.

Mark bumped his arm, "*So*, you come here often, do you?" He laughed.

"Oh, shut it!" Douglas said.

He was still staring up at the entrance of the library. It was as though he had seen an angel. All his life Douglas had believed in angels. Not the kind with wings, but the kind that seemed to drop into his life at the most unlikely times, bringing with them a new beginning. They had appeared so often in his life that he couldn't possibly ignore them anymore. There was the Cub Scout leader who'd remembered his birthday. His high school football coach who'd seen some athletic talent in him. That first college professor, the one who had recognized his creative genius and challenged him to dig deeply into his studies.

Hope had come to him in a similar way—out of the blue, holding another boy's hand and turning around to look at him. She was a vision. Something to behold—and yet something he never felt he could fully grasp, as if she were always just out of reach. It was a fleeting moment, but at the same time it felt permanent. With one look, he was done for. He could see his entire future in her eyes. He knew she would be his wife. And he had been right.

And now, here on the street, in the middle of Fifth Avenue, he had looked into this woman's deep, bright, curious eyes and felt the same. In an instant he saw his past and his future. Both included this woman, Suzy.

After Douglas said his goodbyes to Mark, instead of going back up town, he found a barber shop and asked for a clean shave and new haircut.

Then he headed down to Herald Square, where he turned into Macy's. He bought himself some golf shirts, some khakis, and a new pair of shoes. He suddenly felt the urge to clean up his act. To look presentable. He wanted to look good when he went back to the library the next day. That's where he wanted to be.

Up until he had laid eyes on Suzy, Douglas wasn't sure if he had any "reason to be," as Mark had put it. But he knew now in a way he could not have known when he awoke this morning, that one of *his* reasons to be was named Suzy.

• • •

The next morning, Douglas dressed himself in the new clothes he had bought, removing their tags as he did so. When he was finished, for the first time in months he made his way to the full-length mirror in the walk-in closet and looked at himself.

For being just shy of seventy years old, Douglas felt like a new man. He was surprisingly robust, strong, and youthful looking.

He was in better shape than men half his age. He had broad, sculpted shoulders, strong arms, and long, lean legs. With his new, closely cut hairstyle, Douglas looked more polished than he had in years. Growing up, he always heard that he looked like Sean Connery, and for the first time in his life, he saw the resemblance himself. Perhaps it owed to a little refinement through age.

He took in his reflection as a doctor would examine a patient—assessing and evaluating. If he was being honest with himself, he was in great health. Realizing this, and feeling grateful for it, he did something he hadn't thought he was capable of: Douglas turned the corners of his lips up and smiled. With this miraculous feat accomplished, his entire face lit up in a way Douglas hadn't seen in years. Sure, his eyes crinkled more than they used to in his youth, but they were his eyes all the same. His reflection in the mirror was a person he *recognized*, a person he knew he was capable of being. He was, he realized, coming back to the land of the living.

Douglas had a bounce to his step as he made his way down the stairs and out the door. He sliced quickly through the rush-hour crowds of Fifth Avenue, smiling at strangers and quickly passing by tourists and slower walkers with a polite, "Pardon me."

When he made his way to the foot of the New York Public Library, he suddenly stopped, as if waking from a dream.

"What am I doing?" he mumbled aloud to himself. *I can't just waltz in there and start up a conversation*, he thought.

While he stood staring at the entrance, unbeknownst to Douglas, Suzy appeared beside him.

"Hi. Are you going to go in today, or are you just going to stand there looking at it?" Suzy asked. There was a hint of playful sarcasm in her voice.

Surprised, Douglas looked down beside him and saw her. Today, Suzy was wearing a bright cobalt-blue scarf. She was looking up at him with a bright smile.

"You remembered *me?*" Douglas asked, somewhat astonished.

"Of course I do—we just met *yesterday*." Suzy laughed. "You almost knocked me into Fifth Avenue. Hard to forget that."

"Yes, yes, of course." Douglas laughed along awkwardly. "I am so sorry about that. I wish I could make it up to you."

"Oh, don't be silly; you don't have to make up anything," she replied. "Accidents happen all the time. At least you helped me pick it all up. That counts for something 'round these parts."

"Yes, I suppose it does," Douglas said. "But can I get you a coffee? If you're in a rush, we can get one inside at the library coffee shop?"

"Oh, that's sweet of you," she said. "I'm already running a little late for work, though."

"That's all right. I am on my way in myself. I'll walk in with you. I never got a chance to go in yesterday," he said, walking in step with Suzy.

"What are you in the market for?" she asked.

"Excuse me? What am I *in the market* for?" Douglas asked, confused.

"What *books* are you in the market for? What are you researching, reading, whatever you do here?" she asked. Suzy pointed up at the building as they made their way to the security line.

"Oh, oh, yes of course. I am doing some research about my family," he said so decidedly that it even surprised him.

"Like an Ancestry.com sort of thing?" Suzy asked, opening her bags for the security guard and walking through. "Like your genealogy?"

"No, no. I don't need that exactly. I sort of know where to start looking. I have the clan name McComb or Macomb to work with. It's my last name. I want to know more about my Scottish heritage—see where it takes me.

"I've already taken note of some pretty famous Americans with that name. There was a general in the War of 1812, I think. I have some ancestors who came from Ireland, too, but that's all I have to go on. I grew up not really knowing anything about my past," Douglas said, feeling he had divulged too much. "Well, forget that, that's a story for another day—but now I want to know about my past. I've *got* to know."

"Well, today is your lucky day, Douglas," she said.

"You're telling me," Douglas said with a twinkle in his eye. Running into Suzy today was the luckiest thing that had happened to him for as long as he could remember.

If Suzy had noticed his flirtation at all, she kept it professional. "Well, you're talking to the managing research librarian here," she said. "It's my job to help people research their particular topic— specifically history. I've been giving one-on-one consultations for years. It's literally in my job description, 'to provide specialized subject reference services.'"

"You're kidding?"

"Nope. Once I get up to the desk and get settled, I can help you," she offered.

"That would be great!" Douglas said, beaming. "I'll stay here and get a coffee, and I'll come up and find you. Which room are you in?"

"I am in the Bill Blass Public Catalog Room. Just upstairs. You won't be able to miss me," she said, heading up the large marble staircase. "Give me twenty or so minutes to get settled."

Douglas was absolutely stunned. *How in the world? What were the chances? How was this happening to him?*

He stood in the massive foyer of the library, flanked by two giant staircases. He wondered again, as he had outside the White House all those years ago: *How did I get here?* Only he wasn't only wondering how he had gotten there from the point of view of his heritage, but how he had found himself in this awe-inspiring space about to spend time with a beautiful and intelligent woman, when only months before he couldn't even manage to get out of bed. Life was such a curious thing. How wondrous and capricious and downright baffling that even a chance meeting with a stranger could disrupt his whole world.

Douglas spent the next twenty minutes walking through the gift shop on the main floor, and then he walked through a special exhibit in the main hall about the "Summer of Love." He kept checking his watch. He wanted to honor the twenty minutes Suzy had asked for, but waiting them out felt like an eternity.

When Douglas finally made his way up to the desk, Suzy had put on brightly colored reading glasses. She sat on a high stool behind a large computer. They were eye level with one another now, Douglas noticed.

"Hi, Suzy!" Douglas said, eagerly stepping up to the desk. "Is now an okay time?"

"It's perfect. I actually already got started," she said. "I found out some interesting stuff—just at a cursory glance, but you mentioned knowing that some of your ancestors with the name McComb came over from Ireland, and I found loads of hits on the name John Gordon Macomb Sr., dating back to around 1717. He came here by way of Belfast, Ireland."

"Wow, that was fast!" Douglas said, a slight hint of disappointment edging into his voice. He had hoped for more time with Suzy.

"You sound disappointed," Suzy remarked, noting his demeanor.

"No, no, I think it's great," he said, fumbling slightly. "I want to hear more. Do you know where he came from before that? Do you know who his descendants are? Why did he come here? Are there any books about him?"

Suzy smiled, noting how excited Douglas had become as he rattled off his questions.

"Curiosity is the source of so much joy, isn't it?" Suzy asked rhetorically, looking back at the computer and clicking keys, the blue screen reflecting off her reading glasses.

"I suppose it is." Douglas smiled. "I'll admit it's a bit exciting. Like I'm playing detective."

"You aren't *playing*," Suzy said and stopped typing. She pulled the glasses away from her eyes and perched them on top of her head. "Research is *just like* being a detective. You follow these little bread crumbs that our ancestors leave us, and before you know it, you're following the path back to home. I can't think of anything more exciting. It's why I became a researcher. I love it."

"So you've found your *raison d'être*," Douglas said.

"My 'reason to be,'" Suzy said without missing a beat.

"Everybody needs one," he responded. *Glad Mark wasn't around to hear me say that!* he thought with a chuckle.

"I agree. It makes life so much easier doesn't it?" she said warmly.

Douglas nodded in the affirmative as Suzy clicked away at the keyboard.

"I think this is a great start. Okay, so I can order two books from circulation—seems that they are at another branch. I hate to make you do this, but you'll have to come back when they are ready. Would you mind?"

"Mind? No, I wouldn't mind at all. It would be my pleasure."

"Well, I ordered two books. The first is a general one about famous Scottish Americans that mentions a couple McComb or Macomb men, and the other one is one book specifically about the McComb that came from Ireland to America, which could be one of your ancestors."

"Oh, that would be terrific," Douglas said earnestly. "Thank you."

"I'll just need your library card—or at least be able to look it up," Suzy commented.

Douglas became flustered. "I don't have a library card."

"What?" Suzy asked, incredulous. "I thought that yesterday you said you 'come all the time.'" She eyed him suspiciously.

"I don't come here all the time," he admitted. "Not exactly. You see, I've been meaning to. I just haven't been able to get out much, since my wife. She was sick for a long time, and . . . Well, now I'm alone, and my friend Mark thought it would be good for me to get out and pick up where I left off," Douglas said weakly, feeling unable to fully explain it all.

"That's all right, Douglas. I shouldn't have pried," Suzy said sympathetically. "I didn't mean to upset you. I'm so sorry—truly. Here, why don't you go fill out this form, and I'll get you set up for a library card. In the meantime, I'll order these books for you with my own card, and when they come in, I'll email, and you can come here and we can go through them together. Sound like a plan?" Suzy took off her reading glasses so she could look him in the eyes.

"Yes, that sounds like a wonderful plan." He grabbed the pen and started filling out the form Suzy slid to him.

Inadvertently and still a little flustered, Douglas began to write down his old address—the one he and Hope had shared for so many years. Abruptly he stopped writing and his hand began to shake.

"Douglas?" Suzy asked delicately. "Is everything okay?"

"I'm sorry. I need a new form. I put down the wrong address—my old address," Douglas explained.

"Are you new to the area?" she asked.

"You could say that. I moved into our Manhattan residence up on Fifth Avenue, after . . ." Douglas left the thought unfinished.

"I see," Suzy said, nodding.

"I couldn't bring myself to go back to our home, so I am try-ing out a new city and a new life," he said. "I don't have all the kinks worked out yet." Douglas chuckled to himself, though somewhat wryly.

"Here," Suzy said, taking the pen from his shaking hand. "Why don't you tell me the address and I'll fill it out for you right here online. Since you're a New York City resident, it should be no problem at all. I can even have the card sent directly to you."

"Thank you. You're so kind and patient. New Yorkers get a bad rap sometimes," Douglas said, genuinely grateful.

"Oh, I'm not from around here," Suzy admitted, leaning over to let Douglas in on her secret.

"No? Where are you from?" Douglas asked.

"Virginia," she said. Now that she said so, Douglas realized he could detect the slightest of Southern accents in her speech.

"Ah, explains the Southern hospitality—and the name— *Susannah* Hamilton." Douglas leaned in, looking at her name badge.

"I come from a long line of great Scottish Americans myself," Suzy admitted.

Douglas looked visibly surprised.

"What, because I'm black, I can't be *Scottish*?" she asked, laughing good-naturedly at the naivete of his response. "I might possibly be related to Alexander Hamilton," Suzy continued, a not-undetectable hint of pride in her voice.

"No, no!" Douglas protested, realizing his error. "I mean maybe, but that's not really what I was surprised by—just the coincidence is all. I'm looking into my Scottish-American heritage, trying to figure out if I am related to these great American heroes. And what do you know, you just happen to be doing the same thing— and already know so much.

"It's just that all my life, I've had the most amazing luck. At least I think it's lucky because these perfect people—I call them angels—come in and help me. It's the most amazing thing."

"Well, Douglas, I can assure you, I'm no angel. But I am as close as it gets: I'm a librarian," she said with a laugh.

Douglas laughed with her.

"This has been fun, Douglas, really," Suzy said, smiling. "Such a great way to start my day. But I have so much to do today. Tell you what, I'll order the books right now, and I'll email you as soon as they come in. I'll bet your library card will arrive by then too."

"Yes. Yes, of course. Well, I'll let you get on with it," Douglas said. "Thank you, Suzy, for being so kind and patient with me. I really appreciate it. I look forward to hearing from you!"

"All right, Douglas. You have a great day. I'll be in touch."

"I can't wait," Douglas said, and with that he turned to walk out of the catalog room.

When he got out into the main hall, he looked up at the gorgeous mural painted on the ceiling. The scene was spectacular: Clouds were parting, and behind them brilliant, beautiful light was bursting through the clouds.

Again, Douglas couldn't get over the emotional resonance of the scene before him, the sheer serendipity of it all: For the first time in years, he was indeed seeing the light.

• • •

Several days later, Douglas returned to the library. Just the day before, he had received a computer-generated email stating that his books had arrived and he could pick them up.

Douglas couldn't sleep that night, knowing he was going to see Suzy again. Before he fell asleep he imagined what their conversation might be like the next day, but found himself worrying that she wouldn't be there. *What if she takes the day off and I have to talk to another librarian?* The mere thought of having to talk to someone besides Suzy gave him anxiety. This was all so new. Anything could go wrong. *What if he was wrong about the vibe he felt when he first saw her?* It was so uncharacteristic of him to be so bold—to tell her she had beautiful eyes, to offer his hand? *What if she thought he was coming on too strong, too soon?* He felt almost like a schoolboy. Thoughts of the past—of Hope—crept in to join the chorus of his anxiety as well. *Was it okay for him to even desire another woman? Was it a betrayal of Hope?*

Of course, logically he knew he wasn't betraying anyone with his feelings, but he felt guilty anyway. He knew he had devoted his entire life to Hope. He had even dedicated a memorial in her honor at his alma mater. He loved Hope, he was endlessly devoted to her, and he had taken care of her in a way most men couldn't and wouldn't have done. These are the things he would remind himself of when the sorrow became unbearable.

Now however, in order to buoy himself up from these recent sleepless nights, he thought of Suzy. *What was she like? What interested her? What books did she read? Was she married? Divorced? A widow perhaps?* He had no way of knowing. But he was determined to find out. Yes, he wanted to know where he came from. Sure, he had promised Mark that he would keep himself busy by looking into his ancestry. But suddenly his quest for the past had been usurped by, or in some way been miraculously fused to, the very real present—and maybe to a future filled with possibilities he could hardly have imagined even days ago.

• • •

When Douglas entered the catalog room and saw Suzy, his body relaxed. The worries of the night before instantly dissolved. And when he saw her eyes brighten and her smile widen when she saw him too, he knew that he had not been mistaken.

He confidently walked up to the desk. As he did, a balding man with bifocals stepped forward and said, "I can help you right here, sir."

Douglas balked, but could see that Suzy was presently with another customer.

"That's okay, I'll wait to talk to Suzy," Douglas said.

"Suit yourself," the librarian said curtly. "You could be waiting awhile. Next!"

Douglas stepped aside and let the person standing behind him go on ahead. He was grateful for the wait. He was able to see Suzy in action. He hadn't realized it the first time he saw her, but he could see it now: She was an artist. He wasn't sure what kind—but she had the instincts and taste of a creative person. She had short hair and wore bright, bold earrings. The top she wore was vivid too—full of rich reds, oranges, and yellows swirled in an abstract pattern. It almost looked like a piece of art from the MoMA. To him, it didn't matter what she wore. She looked like sunshine—pure happiness and joy. The outsized warmth and power of the energy she emanated stood in contrast to her small stature. Suzy was petite, easily smaller than most women. She couldn't have been more than five feet tall, Douglas guessed. He took her in from afar and tried to guess her age. He was unsure of it. It didn't look as though she dyed her hair—it was a rich black color, and there were no grays or deep lines in her face. If he had to guess, she was about fifty, but she could easily pass for someone in her early forties. She was fit, healthy, and her light brown skin had a youthful glow. She was, Douglas thought, one of the most beautiful women he'd ever seen.

He must have zoned out while he was staring forward and waiting for his turn, because he hadn't noticed Suzy's customer walk away, nor did he hear Suzy calling for him.

"Yoo-hoo! Hello! Douglas? Are you okay?" Suzy waved from behind the desk.

"Oh, yes, yes! Sorry, I got a little distracted with my own thoughts."

"That's okay. Happens to the best of us. So I take it your books came in?"

"Yes, they did! I am here to pick them up. They should be under *McComb*."

"I remember! Actually, I got a little curious after we talked and did a little more digging of my own," she admitted.

"Really?" Douglas asked, shocked.

"Yes, and I am really interested myself to find out which line you descended from. Either story is equally fascinating!"

"What line? What do you mean? What did you find out?"

"Well," she said excitedly, "follow me."

Douglas watched as Suzy walked from behind the desk and out to greet him on the reading room floor.

"Let's go over here and I can show you," she said. Suzy briskly led the way, gesturing to the row of computers.

She pulled up a chair for herself and one for Douglas in front of one of the consoles.

Douglas sat next to her and smiled.

"You okay?" Suzy asked, puzzled by his expression.

"Oh, yes. Never better." Douglas smiled again. "Curious to find out what happens next."

"Me too," she said, smiling back.

"So what did you find?"

Suzy clicked a few buttons on the computer and brought up an extensive genealogy. "So, the Macombs were a prolific bunch, *if you know what I mean*," she said with a wink.

"I do, ironically enough." Douglas nodded as he looked at the screen before him.

"See all these names that are underlined?" Suzy asked. "Those are links. And each link brings up the lineage and relation of each person.

"So if you click on each link, it will take you as far back as you can go, like this," Suzy demonstrated. "I read about the McComb clan breaking off from the Mackintoshes under someone named Big Thomas, but then I didn't see any hits again until I came across this fellow, John McCooam 'MacCombie'—he's one of the oldest MacCombies, dating back to 1619—pre–Jacobite rebellion, which is amazing," she said.

"Wow, so he's one of my ancestors?" Douglas asked.

"Yes, it seems most lineage charts start with him," Suzy said. "However, the McComb or Macomb clans date back to the Highland clans of the thirteenth century. They were originally part of the Mackintosh clan. It was common back then for clans to split up. The Scottish clans didn't follow primogeniture; they followed the ancient Celtic law of tanistry instead."

"What's that?" Douglas asked.

"It just means that land or property wasn't passed down from father to firstborn," Suzy explained. "It was all about who had the most courage and strength. Anyone in the clan could prove themselves worthy: He who was the strongest took the prize—the land, the cows, the women."

"Wow. Sounds pretty barbaric," Douglas said.

"It was," Suzy agreed. "I know a bit about this from my research into my own past."

"Fascinating," Douglas said.

"It is, and what's really fascinating about your clan's story is that the Mackintoshes ruled an area of land for centuries that the clan leader never visited. This bothered a man named Big Adam, who was the father of Big Thomas. Again, these guys prided themselves on their size and brute force."

"Hence the Highland games," Douglas acknowledged.

"Exactly, but let me go on," Suzy said, eager to get back to her story.

"So, Big Adam raises Big Thomas with these ideas of freedom.

That someone who doesn't step foot on the land shouldn't have a right to claim it, or the women, children, or cattle on it. So as Big Thomas grows up, he wants to make his father proud. And he, too, is sick of wearing the Mackintosh tartan. So one day he declares war on the Mackintoshes. He's ready to be his own man."

"Does he win?"

"He does! He wins and takes the name MacThom. Which over the years became Mac-Om, MaComb, McCombs, or Macomb and several other variations," she said.

"So how did they get from Scotland to here?"

"By boat," Suzy said with a laugh.

"Ha ha, very funny." Douglas poked her gently with his elbow.

"In all seriousness now—they came to this continent by way of Ireland—Belfast."

"So Ireland first?" Douglas asked.

"Yes. A man by the name of John Gordon Macomb Sr. came over in 1717. He is the great-great grandson of John, the one who we have the earliest record of and the descendant of Big Thomas. He had three sons: Alexander and William with his first wife, and then Timothy with an unknown woman. Scandal! His son Alexander Macomb is the founder of the New York Stock Exchange and good friends with my ancestor Alexander Hamilton."

"Well, I'll be damned. That's amazing!" Douglas looked at Suzy in wonder.

"It is, but it's not, in my opinion, nearly as interesting as the next thing I am going to tell you: Timothy, Alexander's half brother, ends up in Canada—on the side of King George. Basically, brother is pitted against brother during the War of 1812—*or so it seems*. But, it turns out Timothy was actually a spy for the Patriots!" Suzy said breathlessly.

"Unbelievable!" Douglas exclaimed. "What about William?"

"Well, I couldn't find much on him," Suzy said.

"So I guess the question is, do I descend from William or Alexander—or Timothy?" Douglas asked.

"Yes, that appears to be your next line of inquiry," Suzy agreed. "In the meantime, you can read the books on the Highlands clans and then the story of John Gordon Macomb, and you can look through all these links. Just keep clicking until you see, say, your father's or grandfather's name. Does that make sense?"

"It does." Douglas nodded. "I think I can do this. My dad wasn't a big talker about our past," Douglas said. He tried to hide the embarrassment he had about his immediate family, certain Suzy could see it all over his face.

If Suzy could sense his shame, she allowed him to save face by ignoring it. "That's okay," she reassured him. "I mean, if you can't, it will still be fun to learn about your entire past, won't it? I mean—either way—you're connected to some serious players in American history."

"I am." Douglas nodded in agreement and excitement. "And, in some ways I'm connected to you, too."

"Oh? How's that?" Suzy asked playfully.

"Well, if you're a Hamilton, I'm assuming you are a descendant from that line—perhaps one of Alexander Hamilton's descendants? And if I descended from Alexander Macomb—our distant relatives would have been friends. And here we are, all these years later, becoming," Douglas trailed off, his uncertainty taking over.

"Friends," Suzy finished Douglas's thought.

"Yes," Douglas said and smiled warmly. "Friends."

"Well, I'll have to look into my own ancestry, to be honest," Suzy confessed. "I'm not even one hundred percent sure how I am related to Alexander Hamilton."

"So we can figure it out together?" Douglas offered, hopeful.

"Yes, I suppose we can. In the meantime, I'll email these links

to you so you can read them in your spare time and follow wher-
ever the trail leads," she added.

"That would be great," Douglas said. "Thank you so much for
all this help. To think that all this time, I've lived my life not knowing all this, not knowing—" Douglas trailed off. He'd wanted to
say, "not knowing *you*," but stopped himself. Things were going
so well, and he wanted them to continue to do so.

"Let's head back to the desk and I'll grab those books for you.
When you're done reading them and looking at those links I sent
you, come on back and we'll look for the next clue," Suzy said.

"You can count on it," Douglas replied.

As Suzy handed the books to him, Douglas took note of her
hands. She wore no ring on her left hand. It suddenly struck
Douglas as so odd that he hadn't even thought to check for this
important detail previously, as infatuated as he had become with
Suzy from the moment he first set eyes on her. But now a smile
spread across his face.

"All right, Suzy. I'll be back soon! Thank you so much for
everything. You really have no idea how much you've helped a
guy out."

"Oh, it's my pleasure, Douglas. It's so exciting to discover
new things, isn't it? Aren't we all just here to keep learning new
things?" Suzy asked wistfully.

"I suppose we are," he said and nodded.

"Good luck, and keep me posted about what you find out!"

"Oh, I will," Douglas said, waving goodbye.

As soon as he got home, he went to his computer and checked
his email.

The first and only email in his inbox was from Suzy. He
opened it immediately and started clicking through the links, and
he proceeded to collect and piece together a loose genealogy.

He was stunned at what he discovered: He knew which line

he came from! Douglas realized that he couldn't wait to go back to the library to tell Suzy. *That* was a new feeling. In fact, for the first time in his life, Douglas felt as if he knew not only where he came from, but also where he was going. And now, he could see Suzy's face no matter which direction he looked.

2

John Gordon Macomb

Fourth Great-grandfather of Douglas McCombs

Born 1717 in Ballyclare, County Antrim, Ireland
Died 1796 in New York, United States

〜

*J*ohn Gordon had never found much enjoyment in the
splendors of youth. His childhood, or lack thereof, was
like that of most young boys whose fathers had wildly
ambitious dreams that they never managed to realize. As the only
surviving son of William and Mary Macomb—who had died
giving birth to a stillborn boy—generations of hopes and dreams
rested on young John Gordon's shoulders.

His father William, also an only son, had felt the same sense
of urgency during his own childhood. William's father, John Jr.,
wanted nothing more than for his son William to be successful,
make him proud, and live free—messages he impressed upon
young William at every opportunity. These, of course, were
the messages his father, John Macomb Sr., a Scotsman, had
passed on to him. John Sr. came from a long line of Scots, each
of whom had believed that a man's worth was determined by
the courage of his convictions, his commitment to staying the
course, and his ability to deliver results—in other words, "to
be a free man." John Sr. himself had been raised with stories
about his own ancestors. His third great-grandfather Douglas
and his third great-uncle Thomas regaled the family with tall
tales of their Scottish clan ancestry. John Sr. had descended from
Big Thomas—a rebel and free man. He'd been an ambitious
man who protected his family's honor by throwing off the yoke
another man sought to keep him under.

John Sr. passed these stories on to John Jr., who passed them
on to William, who passed them on to John Gordon as soon as
he was old enough to sit through their telling without squirming.
This, then, was how John Gordon learned of great wars and battles between Highland clans—usually over land and who had the
ownership of it. He learned early and often that so much of a man's
identity in this world depends on what that man owns and who or
what owns that man. It was also during these conversations that

he learned of the profound opportunity to change one's destiny that could be had simply by changing one's land.

The first time the notion occurred to him was over dinner.

"Da, why did your grandfather John leave Scotland for Ireland if he loved it so much?" he asked.

"Well, John Gordon, you can love something very much but still have to leave it," his father replied. "Sometimes there is a cause much greater than love."

"What's that?" John Gordon asked, his brow furrowed in confusion.

"Freedom," his father said simply.

"I don't understand, Da."

"You see, in the sixteenth century, there was an English king, Henry VIII. He decided to seize all the land of Ireland and make it his own," William explained. "He could rule the land and take all the riches and food from it that he wanted."

"Doesn't seem fair," John Gordon said.

"Well, it wasn't if you were Irish," William said, winking.

"So he sends in his troops and his people, and word spreads from all the Gael clans that the king is seizing land. This rumor gets back to the Highlands, of course. Now, the Scottish and Irish have a tricky history of their own, but when it comes to the notion of freedom, we've always been on the same team, do you understand?"

"I think so. What you're saying is that the Irish clans called on their Scottish friends for a favor," John Gordon offered.

"You could say that," William replied, nodding. "But, clans being clans, not everyone was always on the same side. Still, most Scottish Highlanders didn't think it was right—on principle. Scotland has a long history, dating all the way back to William Wallace in the thirteenth century, of doing everything they can to fight off English control," William said.

"So the Scots and Irish wanted to be free from England?" John Gordon asked.

"Well, yes and no," William replied. "Folks will be arguing about that one for centuries to come. Some want to be under control; others don't. Hence the endless wars. Rest assured this is an argument that will be debated for centuries—long after you and I are gone. In fact, the fight went on for years and years between the Gaels and the Brits. By the time Henry VIII's daughter, Queen Elizabeth I, wore the crown, the English were still trying to take land from the Irish, and the Scottish were still sending in reinforcements to help."

"Oh, I know about Elizabeth—the Virgin Queen!" John Gordon said excitedly. "I learned about her in school!"

"Yes, well, she was no virgin saint to the Irish, I assure you," William scoffed. "She sent English forces to occupy the northeast corner of Ireland—Ulster—to create a barrier between the Gaels of Ireland and the Highlanders of Scotland. The English didn't want any Scottish mercenaries or warriors coming in to help the Irish, but the MacDonnell clan of Ireland called for reinforcements from the Scottish Highlands all the same—and they came in droves."

"Our ancestors, the MacThomases, were from the Scottish Highlands," John Gordon said excitedly, piecing the story together. "Did they help the Irish fight off the English?"

"I think so," William replied. "But they weren't successful. Around five hundred Irish civilians were massacred by the English forces, and it left a lasting hatred for the English crown in both the Irish and Scottish peoples."

"I can see why," John Gordon said pensively. After sitting quietly for some time, he spoke up again. "You know, Da, all this fighting seems so silly. It seems like a waste for so many men to fight and die for an idea, even one like freedom." The boy shook his head.

"What did you say, John Gordon?" William asked, his voice suddenly deadly serious. "What did you say?"

John Gordon looked down at his porridge. "I just said it seems silly—"

"*Bite your tongue, boy!*" William cut him off. "No child of mine will *ever* say such a thing! Do you know whose blood was shed so you could sit here today and eat that porridge?"

John Gordon bowed his head and said nothing. He looked at his own hands, blistered and bloodied from the work he had done on their farm. *My own blood*, he thought, though he dared not speak his thought aloud.

William followed his son's gaze and worked out what was on the boy's mind. "You think you're tough?" William's voice was raised now. "You think because you *bleed* a little doing a day's work, you're *tough*?"

"No, sir," John Gordon said quietly.

"How would you feel if I stole that porridge you worked so hard for?" William continued, louder still. "How would you feel if took your *clothes*? This *house*?"

John Gordon pursed his lips. His face was growing hot and red under the pressure of his father's interrogation. "I'd be mad!" John Gordon yelled, meeting William's booming ferocity with the squeaking outrage of a young boy.

"You're damn right you'd be mad!" William hollered back. "You've got to *fight* to keep what's yours, and you gotta help others fight for their right to do the same! *Do you understand, son?*"

"Yes, Da," John Gordon said, nodding, and silence fell between them again. It was a long while before John Gordon felt brave enough to ask another question.

"If all the Irish were killed, Da, then why did our ancestors stay in Ulster? Why didn't they just go back to the Highlands?" the boy asked.

"Well, John Gordon, that's another life lesson for you," William answered. "They stayed for the *opportunity*."

"What?" John Gordon asked, perplexed.

"Freedom is great. It's noble. It's the basis for everything else, namely something called *opportunity*," William explained. "The two go hand in hand, and don't you ever forget it.

"By the time the fighting was over, the English were motivated to prevent further violence by offering their former Scottish enemies land rights to plantations all over northern Ireland," William explained. "So the Scots had a real opportunity to make money, have their own land, and live near friends with shared values. Why would they leave? When you have freedom and opportunity, son, anything is possible. *Anything*."

John Gordon nodded, but at ten years old, he didn't truly understand what his father meant—not for many years to come. He would revisit his memory of that conversation again and again as he grew up, to consider the meaning of *freedom* and *opportunity*. In time, both would become driving forces in his life.

• • •

By the time he was fifteen, John Gordon had witnessed the death of his mother and the gradual unraveling of his family as once-vigorous William began to fade completely into oblivion, slowly drinking himself to death out of grief. It seemed that the wild-eyed dreamer John Gordon had so adored listening to as a young boy was gone, having never fully recovered from the death of his young wife. Ultimately, John Gordon had no choice but to watch as William became increasingly reclusive and despondent. For all his talk of freedom and opportunity, in the end John Gordon's father could never be truly free himself. In the years following the loss of his wife, he was chained to his suffering. He couldn't eat. He couldn't work. All he could do was numb himself with drink, incapable of feeding and providing for his young son.

John Gordon learned then, as so many poor and underprivileged children do, that necessity is indeed the mother of invention. At a young age, John Gordon needed to quickly learn how to grow his own food, and even how to cook for both his father and himself. Driven by hunger and the desire to be free, financially speaking, John Gordon also figured out ways to make money. As the first of a long line of entrepreneurs, John Gordon grew vegetables and sold them at the market. When he had accrued money this way, he bought food wholesale from other farms and peddled it at the markets to turn a profit. Then, he turned his interest to textiles and other serviceable goods. He became a master at importing cheaply and selling at a considerable profit.

As a wealthy and ambitious—not to mention large and good-looking—man, John Gordon was the most eligible bachelor in the county. So when it came time to marry, he had his choice of lasses. Mothers and fathers from several counties dreamed that their daughters would marry such a driven, ambitious, and obviously successful man. For his part, though, John Gordon had eyes on only one girl, Jane, whom he believed to be the most exciting person in Ballyclare, and the only woman who could match his industriousness.

Jane sold wool in the same market where John Gordon sold textiles, working alongside her widowed mother. Jane was strong, fearless in her work, sharp with finances, and boldly outspoken, too. If anyone tried to cheat her out of a sale, she would give them a real tongue-lashing. She had wild red hair, green eyes, and though she was a small woman, she was both fierce and strong. Occasionally, John had to wrangle with her himself when he was in the market for wool, and she always got a little more out of him than anyone else.

When he screwed up the nerve to ask for her hand in marriage, John Gordon knew his proposal would have to be an earnest, if unromantic, one. An almost businesslike proposal would best befit Jane's no-nonsense proclivities.

"If you marry me, we can combine our markets and open a shop together," he told her. "We can build a home, and I can take care of your mother. We could be the richest family in Ballyclare." He had approached her with the proposal one day in the market, bearing a modest handful of heather and the ring his mother had given him shortly before her death. On his way to ask for Jane's hand in marriage, he had recalled his own mother's last words: "Take this ring, John Gordon. Hide it from your Da. He'll want to pinch it and sell it for drink. I want you to have it and give it to *a girl that you'll take care of.*"

John Gordon hadn't understood what she had meant when he was just a small boy. He hadn't known that she was dying. She had been bedridden for some time, but such was often the case in those times with women in the last months of pregnancy. Though John Gordon didn't appreciate the importance of his mother's final gift to him, he did as she instructed and hid the ring. From the moment he saw Jane, he knew she was the one the ring had been intended for—though he also knew that Jane certainly didn't need any *taking care of.*

"You're a fool, John Gordon!" Jane said, once he had handed her the flowers and the simple gold band. "A romantic fool!"

"So does that mean you'll be my wife?" he asked.

"Yes," she said with a laugh. "But that doesn't mean you'll be getting a discount on today's wool."

"Of course not. I wouldn't dream of it—not until we're married," John Gordon said and laughed himself.

Several weeks later, John Gordon and Jane were married, and

soon after, they had not only opened Belfast's most popular mercantile, but Jane was pregnant as well.

Over the long months of Jane's pregnancy, John Gordon began to be beset with worries and fears. Fear overtook his entire body. *What if I lose her? What if she dies like my own mother?* He was riddled with foreboding and anxiety. He couldn't think. He couldn't concentrate at work. He couldn't sleep. The mere thought of losing Jane in childbirth—the same way his own mother had died—had left him positively distraught.

Jane tolerated none of it. "I am small but strong, I assure you, John Gordon. My mother was near my size, and she managed to bear me and live to raise me besides."

John Gordon's love for his wife took deeper root with each passing day. As he watched her belly grow, he tried his best to keep at bay the terror and panic that threatened to seize his heart at every moment.

When Jane gave birth to their son, Alexander, John Gordon was astounded by her strength and resolve. With each successive child—a boy, William, and a girl called Anne—John Gordon's love and admiration for his wife only intensified.

Jane was an astonishment: She helped him with management and running of the mercantile, kept the books, and raised and taught his children. With her help, encouragement, and willfulness, John Gordon, at a mere thirty-eight years of age, had amassed a sizeable fortune. He was now one of the most successful men on Bridge Street in Belfast, and he owed Jane every success. In fact, he often said so aloud to customers, clients, and anyone who congratulated him on his success.

"Oh, it's not me," he would say with a deferential smile. "Jane should get all the credit."

And so, sitting in his beautifully appointed office on Bridge

Street and watching the British Royal Army's ships as they sailed in and out of Belfast Harbour, John Gordon almost felt guilty for wanting more—for being bored with his lot. *There has to be more. There must be*! he thought. For as long as he could remember, John Gordon could hear his father's words: *freedom and opportunity*. He could not let go of the thought, either, that there was simply so much to be had from a sprawling new land an ocean away.

The word was out, the British Army was being sent over to keep control of this New World that the pesky French wanted a piece of as well. John Gordon knew what that meant for him and his business. *The Royal Army would be in need of supplies*. He had made his fortune in Belfast by seizing similar opportunities—procuring and supplying the particular needs of particular people at a particular time—and now there was no better market than a standing army. *Ah, the opportunities*, John Gordon thought.

All these years later, John Gordon still thought it was all so silly, same as he had back when his father had first told him the ill-fated stories of the Scots' desire for independence, fighting and dying for freedom from the English. Nobody ever won that war. Hadn't people learned their lesson? For centuries the Scottish and Irish had been defeated. And now the French thought they could best the Crown and divest them of their American colonies? Unbelievable! *Well, if the French aren't going to learn their lesson, at least I can seize the opportunity and free myself financially in the process*, John Gordon thought. *There is a great deal of money to be made in the Americas, a very great deal, and I know just how to do it.*

There was only one problem: Jane.

John Gordon knew his wife. It would be difficult to persuade Jane to leave behind her beloved home and the business she had helped him build. She was predictable, liked things to stay the same, and loved a good routine. Her life was ordered and dull, just the way she liked it. John Gordon also knew she wouldn't want to risk the children's lives—taking them across the wide ocean to a whole new, far less civilized land.

But he could see it all so clearly: their success, the ability to start a dynasty of their own in a new colony. And when the British inevitably won the war? His mind overflowed with visions of the accolades he would receive, the financial rewards he'd be given—he might even be awarded some land and become a lord! He could rise from living in a shack in Belfast to being a lord over untold tracts of bounteous land in a brand-new colony. *Freedom! Opportunity!* He was wont to burst with anticipation and excitement.

Later that evening, after the servants had cleared their tea and had taken the children to bed, John Gordon made the second of the two most important proposals of his life to Jane. Just as he had when he'd asked for Jane's hand, he needed to be pragmatic, to appeal to her logical sensibilities, when he made this proposal.

"Jane, I've come upon an opportunity, and we simply must pursue it. I have had a realization that there is so much more money to be made in this life than could ever be had at the market. In fact, with what I've heard about the new colonies, the potential for prosperity seems limitless," John Gordon began.

"Don't you dare say it, John Gordon," Jane cut him off with no sign of good humor. "I know what you're going to say. Every wife in town is fighting with her husband tonight over this harebrained idea. Every man in town heard the same foolishness from their fathers growing up. You've always been smarter than that, John Gordon! I love how smart you are. I do. I love how ambitious you are. That's what I love about you. But please, don't ask this of me." She looked her husband dead in the eye. A proud woman, pleading did not come naturally to Jane. "Please," she said quietly, softening her manner.

"Why not?" John Gordon pressed her. "Jane, can you not imagine the opportunities? The British will surely keep their claims there. The French have no stronghold. And if we get there and do great work for the Crown, imagine the land we could acquire—the status? Our sons could go to King's College; our daughter could marry a general. I could be a lord and you a lady! Imagine it: You and I—two hardworking beggars sitting side by side with royals! If you cannot want it for yourself, can you for our children, and our children's children, and our children's children's children?"

"You're a fool, John Gordon," Jane said. It was the same answer she'd given when he had proposed marriage all those years ago, and in that moment John Gordon knew that he and his family were on their way to the British Colonies. He had persuaded her.

"You will not regret this, Jane. You will not ever, ever regret this."

"I hope you're right," she said, rising from her chair. She stood behind him and draped her arms around his neck, kissing him on the cheek. "I believe that we have only made it this far because we've been together, and I don't see that there is anything we can't achieve so long as we stay together."

John Gordon never thought he could love his wife more than the day he married her, and he had felt the same after she gave birth to their first child. But his love had continued to intensify again and again after the second and third were born. Every day she surprised him, and every day she gave him a new reason to love her even more.

But in this moment now, with her arms wrapped tightly around him and her voice assuring him of their success, John Gordon felt an overwhelming sense of love and gratitude for Jane that he had never before imagined possible. He couldn't imagine there would ever come a time when he wouldn't love her with his entire being. He couldn't imagine anything ever coming between them.

All he could see was success—freedom, opportunity, and love. It was all a man needed to be happy. And more than ever before, he was sure of two things: Nothing would ever come between him and Jane, and the British would win this war and guarantee him and his progeny untold riches for generations to come.

• • •

By 1765, John Gordon had proved himself to be quite the fortune teller—at least when it came to business. Though he hadn't received formal orders to move to Albany some years before, John Gordon had sensed it was the best place for him to be. He could never truly account for what had made the decision for him. Had it been intuition? Luck? Some well-timed advice he couldn't quite remember? Regardless, many would argue that his choice to move his business to Albany at the dawn of the Seven Years' War was one of the best financial decisions of his life—albeit his last.

For yes, by the end of the war in 1963, Macomb was one of the most prosperous men in the region, supplying officers with all manner of goods—not just textiles and uniforms, but expensive luxury goods like telescopes, books, snuff, and wine and spirits. He even became county judge.

His life was seemingly perfect. His wife loved him. He was successful, and his children were growing up to be fine people. In fact, his eldest son, Alexander, was now seventeen years of age and preparing to leave home to strike out on his own in search of freedom and opportunity.

But just then, John Gordon—a man in the prime of his life and at the height of his success—heard a knock at the door.

• • •

John Gordon and his wife Jane listened from the parlor as a servant went to the door to receive their unexpected guest.

"I am here to speak to John Gordon Macomb," a woman said softly.

"He's in the parlor. I will get him for you," the servant replied. "May I ask who's calling?"

"No, he won't come if he knows it's me," the young woman replied, her voice trembling.

"You wait here, miss," the servant said, closing the door and leaving the girl outside. She headed back to the parlor. "Mr. Macomb, sir," the servant said deferentially. "There is a woman here to see you."

"Well, send her in," Jane said defiantly, ignoring the fact that the servant had addressed her husband. "It's freezing out."

The servant hesitated and looked at John Gordon pleadingly. While a dull sense of familiarity had dawned on him when he'd heard the voice of their unexpected guest, the moment John Gordon saw the look on the servant girl's face, he knew instantly who was at the door.

"No!" John Gordon said a little too forcefully. He stood up. "No, I'll go speak with her. She's just a crotchety old customer I had to send out of the store earlier today. She refuses to pay her bill. She's probably come to sweet talk me out of it."

"Well, don't let her off the hook," Jane said, returning to her needlepoint.

"Wouldn't dream of it," John Gordon replied. He smiled nervously.

As soon as he'd opened the door and confirmed the identity of the woman now standing on the porch, John Gordon stepped outside and closed the door behind him.

"What are you *doing* here?" he whispered curtly.

"You haven't returned my letters, John," the girl replied, helplessness in her voice. "It's almost my time and I need to know what to do." She wrapped her arms around herself against the cold, her swollen belly straining against an old, threadbare coat that had never been intended to accommodate a woman with child.

"Well, you don't come to my home where my wife and children live!" he snapped.

"I have nowhere else to go!" the girl argued back. "I don't know what to do, and the baby will be here in a month!"

"How do I even know it's mine?" John Gordon said contemptuously. "How do I know you're not just after my money?"

"But John Gordon!" The girl's eyes were shining with tears, and her voice cracked as she spoke. "I *love* you. You love me."

"Shh!" John chided the girl, his eyes wild. "Woman, my *wife* is inside!"

At that the door opened.

Jane stood in the doorway, and as she took in this sorry scene, both John Gordon and his pregnant mistress knew their secret was out. Jane could see the whole story clear as day from the guilty look in John Gordon's eyes and the girl's belly already heavy with child, though she looked to be no more than a child herself.

Jane let the rage wash over her for a long moment before resigning herself to do what she always did with her feelings: put them aside to get to the business at hand.

"John Gordon, please invite your young friend in the house," she said, cold and businesslike. "You're letting all the heat out."

She stepped aside and let the couple slink past her into the house. The young woman turned and looked back at Jane apologetically.

"This way." Jane raised her hand to point toward the parlor. "Please, sit. Would you like some tea?"

John Gordon couldn't abide this—his wife and his young lover sitting side by side. He paced the room.

"John, please sit down," Jane said, her voice deadly calm.

His wife never ceased to surprise him. John Gordon had no

idea what she was about to say or do. All he knew for certain was that she knew exactly what he had done with this woman, and what their affair had wrought. Jane was no fool. It was John Gordon who was the romantic. He was the one who made pronouncements of love. But she was the one who *showed* love. She was steadfast, strong, and resolute. *And yet everyone has their limits*, he thought. She could leave him and take the children, even his fortune. She could ruin his good name.

"So it seems we have a baby on the way," Jane said.

The woman nodded nervously. Her eyes darted to John Gordon, seeking an ally in this strange circumstance she found herself in. He would not look at her.

"And you are not married?" Jane asked, looking stone-faced at John Gordon as she did.

"No, I am not," the young woman replied. She stared down at her hands, resting gingerly on her belly, afraid to look Jane in the eyes.

"And do you have any intention of caring for this child on your own?" Jane asked.

"I—I—I am unsure of what to do. I'd like to give this child the best chance they can, but if they're a basta—"

"Now, now, now," Jane cut the girl off primly. "Don't say such a thing. The child has no choice in such matters. The way I see it, there's no reason children should pay for their father's mistakes by carrying such an awful label their whole lives."

She was talking to the girl, but Jane stared coldly at John Gordon as she spoke. "Now as far as I can tell, there *is* a logical solution to this . . . dilemma. I am married. I am John Gordon's wife. *I* will raise the child," Jane said matter-of-factly, to the astonishment of both her husband and his young lover. "I have three other children. I can care for and love this one as my own, so you can go off and find a *respectable* man to marry and have children with when you are older and wiser."

John was stunned. His jaw went slack in shock.

"But, Jane!" he protested. "I couldn't ask you to do such a thing!"

Jane inhaled deeply to collect herself against the rage building inside her. When she had regained control of herself, she spoke again, sharply, in measured sentences. "No, you couldn't ask me, *could you?* But you *could* ask me to sit by while you defiled our marriage bed. You could ask me to sanction your relationship with a mere *child*, a girl no older than your own son. You *could* ignore my feelings, your children's feelings. You *could* risk all of our reputations. You *could* play me for a fool." Jane nearly spat the last line at her husband, such was her anger, but she took another moment to gather herself.

"But you, John Gordon," she continued, calmer now though no less angry, "no, you *couldn't possibly ask me* to care for an innocent child. You are a fool, John Gordon Macomb! You have always been a fool, a damn romantic fool. Chasing after freedom, oppor-tunity—*love.* You speak of love as if you know what it is! Is this love?" She pointed to the young woman's belly, though John Gordon could barely bring himself to look. "Is *this* love?" Jane pointed now at her husband, cowering in his chair like a child. "You don't know *anything* about love. You don't know what it's like to care for something, tend to it, watch it grow, and then have to watch it slipping from you constantly, because *that something that you love* always wants something more, extra, better, newer. You wanted a mercantile, then you wanted a bigger one. Then you wanted a new country. Now you have a new girl. Well, lucky you! You have it all now, don't you, John Gordon?" The white-hot fire of her rage now spent, Jane regarded her husband coldly.

"Jane, Jane, I am so sorry. Please," John Gordon begged, his eyes red and shining.

"I should go!" the girl said, standing up abruptly.

"Sit down!" Jane said firmly and put her hand on the girl's

shoulder to push her back into her seat. The girl could not resist her. "You will do no such thing. You will remain here, in this home. We will care for you, and when the child is born, we will care for it. It is settled. I will fetch the servants."

Jane rose and walked from the room to summon the servants. John Gordon chased her, abandoning his young lover to sit nervously in the parlor.

"You can't be serious! You want to let *that woman* live with us, Jane? To raise her child?" John asked, aghast.

"*That woman? Her* child?" Jane hissed, spinning to face her husband. "*Her* child? Have you gone mad, sir? Do you not know how this works? *You* are the baby's father. This child will bear your name for generations. And so we will raise it as our own."

With that, Jane turned again to walk back down the hall toward the servants' quarters, leaving her husband behind her. John Gordon shook his head. His wife was an unfathomable mystery. But, as he so often proclaimed to himself, again he found that he loved her more in that moment than he had ever loved her before.

This time when the thought occurred to him, so did another: Jane's brand of love—steady, forceful, resolute love—would be the kind he would from now on be obliged to return to her until the day he died. He did not know what he had done to deserve such a remarkable woman, but he was profoundly grateful for her all the same.

When Timothy Macomb was born, Jane fulfilled her promise. She took the squalling child from the arms of his dead mother and from that day forward loved him as her own.

Timothy's father and siblings—Alexander, William, and Anne—would find that more difficult to do.

3

WE HAVE
RESEARCH TO DO!

*D*ouglas put down the book he had just finished about John Gordon Macomb and pulled off his reading glasses. He rolled over in bed to yank his reading lamp's light switch off. For several moments he sat in the dark, staring at the sliver of light cracking through the curtains that created a long streak across the empty space beside him in bed.

What's it like to see one's own life in a book? he thought. *To see one's life in the past? In one's own ancestors? How is it that so many traits of an ancestor could still exist all these centuries later?* No matter how hard he tried to shut off the thoughts, he couldn't shake all the musings that the book had provoked within him. Amazing how a string of words could take such hold over a person, immerse him in another world, and at the same time transform his present one.

Since Douglas had left Suzy at the library, he had read about his Highland ancestors and his fourth great-grandfather, John Gordon Macomb, not to mention his third great-uncle and third great-grandfather—the half brothers, sons of an ambitious dreamer and a romantic—grandsons of an alcoholic. Douglas couldn't get over the many similarities between himself and John Gordon. John Gordon was an entrepreneur like him. He too was a romantic who adored his wife. Douglas thought of his own father—and shook his head at the memories, the deeply held secrets and shame. He thought of John Gordon's sons—William, Alexander, and Timothy, and what had become of them—the different paths the brothers ultimately took, and he thought of his own siblings. When he thought of them, immediately he felt shame. It was all too much to bear—*to remember*.

How could he ever tell Suzy such things?

But the books were due in the morning. He wanted to see Suzy, but he dreaded her inquiries about what he had discovered. He could imagine what she would ask, and fear rose up inside him. *What if she thinks I am crazy? What if she hears about my life and runs for the hills?* Perhaps it was best, Douglas considered as he tried to get to sleep, if one just left the past in the past.

When the alarm went off the next morning, Douglas realized he had never slept at all. The book had ignited too many memories. It was the first book he had dared to read in years. He had refrained from doing so, because reading was too hard. It conjured too many memories. Yes, it was a dangerous thing to read when one was so susceptible to remembering. Now, thanks to the book's spell, he was entranced and had no other choice but to remember. He remembered his childhood, his courtship with Hope. He remembered how romantic he had been, much like John Gordon before him. He remembered how he adored Hope. The flowers he brought to her, the notes he left her, the gifts he lavished over her. He thought about how he loved her more and more as each day passed, as John Gordon loved his Jane, and that that love was simply never enough. Not for Hope, anyway.

That's when he remembered *the indiscretion*—the thing that almost broke Jane and John Gordon. Thinking about Jane's pain and her indignity at such a revelation, Douglas tried hard to fight back the wellspring of memories rising up within him. He wanted to stop them. It was too much to bear—for any man to bear. He thought of Jane, her resolve and her noble response to her husband's infidelity, and his stomach knotted. *Please not now. Please not now. I don't want to remember any of it. Not now.* He feared closing his eyes because of what he might see when the thoughts finally came. There was no end to them. He tried to get ahead of them, but it was of no use.

Douglas's mind had a mind of its own.

By the time he roused himself from the bed, he was exhausted. He was in no mood to talk to anyone. He felt depressed, as he often did after restless nights. *What was the point of it all? Living? Breathing? Finding out what happened in* the *past if it was all going to end eventually? If it was all going to just amount to the same result? What was the point of wanting more, and being more, and loving more—if love just ended?*

Reluctantly Douglas dressed, made himself a coffee, and sat alone in his kitchen staring at the books he needed to return.

Speaking aloud to the empty room, he asked, "What have I done? What have I opened up?"

There was no answer, of course, as Douglas was alone. He had been alone for months now, and nothing he said or did or discovered about his past was going to change that reality.

Douglas resigned himself to this thought, grabbed the books off the kitchen table, and headed out of the house.

"To hell with it," he said to himself.

Walking toward the library, Douglas was sure he was going to drop the books off and tell Suzy he was done with this nonsense. It was foolish of him to think finding out where he was from was going to give him any peace now. He was just delaying the inevitable. He was alone, and he was going to die alone. Why bring another person into his ridiculous melodrama?

However, when he stepped into the library and saw Suzy again in person, it was as if he had awakened from a bad dream. He realized that all those negative thoughts had been exacerbated by his lack of sleep. He was just being cranky and irrational. He now felt a sense of joy when Suzy's eyes lit up as he approached her.

"Douglas! You're back! How are you?" she said excitedly.

Hesitant to answer with some meaningless pleasantries because it felt so disingenuous, Douglas shrugged.

"Douglas? Are you okay? Do you need to sit down?" Suzy asked, while moving around the desk toward him. "You don't look well."

"Oh, I just had a rough night's sleep," Douglas said, closing his eyes and waving her off with his hand.

"I am about to go on a break. Why don't we step out and get some air?" she asked.

Douglas looked stunned. "You want to spend your break—with me?"

"Sure, let's go sit outside by the fountain," Suzy said, smiling. "You look like you could use some fresh air." She took Douglas by the arm and guided him out of the room.

It had been so long since anyone had taken care of him that Douglas was unsure how to respond. He simply let her lead the way out of the grand foyer and down the stairs.

"Would a cappuccino be okay?" Suzy asked.

"Wait, you're getting me a coffee?" Douglas asked.

"Yes, my treat."

Douglas smiled and said, "No, no, no. Let me pay."

"Oh, don't be silly. It's a coffee, not a house."

Douglas watched as Suzy paid and walked back with two cappuccinos in hand.

"Let's find a spot by one of the fountains," she said, once again leading the way.

Douglas followed her and was quietly amazed at the turn of

events. *Imagine if he hadn't come? Imagine if he had given up? How close is each of us to missing out on something wonderful?* He pondered the fate underlying such questions as he took his seat beside her.

"So, what did you find out?" Suzy said, sipping the frothy milk of her cappuccino.

"Too much, really," Douglas said.

"Like?"

"Like, my fourth great-grandfather John Gordon, the one who came from Ireland, is more like me than I care to think about."

"Oh? How's that?"

"He was an entrepreneur—a successful one."

"That doesn't seem so terrible," Suzy said.

"He was inventive out of necessity—he had a rough childhood," Douglas said, tightening up his lower lip, trying to hold back emotion.

"Oh." Suzy nodded. "And, I am guessing you did too?"

"It wasn't easy." Douglas nodded.

"How was your life like John Gordon's?"

"We both had similar fathers—big dreamers, big talkers when it came to freedom, love, and doing great things. Both men left a lot to be desired. John Gordon's father relied a lot on him to run the farm and provide for the family. I could relate to that. I grew up in a shack. We had no running water. We knew hunger, and we lived a day-to-day existence. We didn't even have an outhouse. We used a bucket in the corner of the room. Very rudimentary," Douglas said, wrinkling his nose in disgust at the memory.

Suzy nodded in recognition.

"As you can imagine, we didn't have much. If I wanted something—to wear or eat—I had to figure out a way to get it. Just like John Gordon."

"Isn't that interesting?" Suzy asked.

"Interesting?" Douglas said, his eyes widening. "I bare my soul and you say it's *interesting*?" He let out a little laugh.

"I don't mean any offense. It's just that despite both of your impoverished upbringings and rough childhoods, you both became successful—I mean, you're wearing Ferragamo shoes." She pointed to Douglas's feet. "You're no slouch, Douglas."

Douglas let out a laugh. "You don't miss a detail, do you?"

"I know how to read the tea leaves, if you know what I mean," she said with a wink.

"Oh yeah? And what do you read about me?" Douglas asked, leaning back as if to give her a better look.

"I see a devoted man, someone who worked hard his whole life—and from the looks of it, doesn't need to worry about money or where his next paycheck is coming from anymore," she said, studying him. "He's got enough time on his hands—at a fairly young retirement age—to read books and do research. He wants to know where he came from and how he got to where he is. He's probably pretty successful and wants to know where all that success came from." Suzy looked for his reaction. "How am I doing so far?" she asked with a smirk.

"Wow, you can really read a guy." Douglas smiled.

"But I don't know everything. I mean, I may have been wrong about a couple of things at first," Suzy admitted.

"Oh? Like what?"

"Truth be told, I thought you were just another rich guy. It was your fancy shoes—that's what I noticed when I was bending over to pick up all the things I dropped from my purse—you know, when you and your friend bumped into me. That guy—" Suzy searched her memory for the name of the man Douglas was with when they first met.

"Mark?" Douglas added.

"Yes, Mark! He looked like a banker type. Rich guys always

walk around with banker types. It wasn't fair, but I guess I had you typecast. I figured you had been born to wealth and stayed that way," she said, shaking her head.

Douglas let out a laugh. "I can assure you I was not born rich. Those early days were rough."

"I see. But look where you are now!" Suzy said hopefully, patting Douglas's arm, letting it linger a moment. When Douglas reached out to return her touch, Suzy seemed nervous and pulled away. Trying to be more professional, she hastily returned the conversation back to Douglas's ancestry.

"So, were you able to find your father's name on those links and connect him back to one of John Gordon's sons?" Suzy asked.

"Yes, but it's not who I was hoping for, to be perfectly honest with you." Douglas shook his head.

"Oh? Why's that?"

"I was hoping to be a descendant of Alexander Sr., the great Revolutionary War hero and friend to Alexander Hamilton and founder of the New York Stock Exchange. It would mean that, I don't know, somehow you and I . . ."

"Would have a connection?" Suzy finished Douglas's thought.

"Yes, exactly," Douglas said with a bit of an exhalation.

Suzy nodded. "I understand. I was hoping for that too."

"Really?" Douglas said, but before he could finish his thought, Suzy interjected.

"It doesn't matter, though. Right? Whether we were connected in the past, because we're connected now?"

"Ha! I guess so, but wouldn't it have been something if your ancestor and my ancestor were friends?"

"Oh, whether it was your third great-grandfather or uncle, we're still connected, right? I mean, their stories all entwined in a way, right? And they lived in the past? I mean, the stories all overlap already, don't they?"

"True," Douglas agreed.

"I mean, take my history, for example," she began as Douglas leaned over to listen intently. "I didn't have it easy either."

"That's right," Douglas said. "I've been talking so much about my life, please tell me about yours."

"Well, I was raised by a single mother. She adored me and protected me—a little too much. She worked hard to provide for me, put me through school—it was tough, but not 'a-sewage-bucket-in-the-living-room kind of tough,'" Suzy said with a laugh.

"Still, it sounds like it wasn't easy?" Douglas asked softly.

Reaching for her coffee and staring at it, Suzy nodded without saying another word.

"Your mom, she had a lot of expectations? Demands, I gather?" Douglas asked.

"That's one way to put it," she said with a small laugh.

"Had control issues?" Douglas asked.

"Yes. Though in a way, I don't blame her. Her husband, my father, ran off when I was young. I was all she had. And she had no one else to help her. In so many ways, it makes sense. As much as we want to forget our past or act as if it doesn't impact our present, there is no ignoring the truth of it," Suzy said.

"And what's the truth of it?" Douglas asked.

"That we are, in so many ways, bound by our past. Prisoners, if you will, so long as we don't acknowledge it and make things right," Suzy added.

"But, how do you do that—how do you become free of the past once and for all?" Douglas asked earnestly, thinking about the long, sleepless nights in which he felt imprisoned and bedeviled by his own thoughts.

"Freedom isn't just a mere concept. It's real. It's a thing. *An actual thing*. It can be taken from you. It can be stolen, usurped. And our pasts are real—and they can steal our freedom, like a thief in the night. Our lives can be stolen by the greed of others. Our land, our property, our bodies can be, too," Suzy trailed off.

Douglas nodded in agreement. "People die every day just wanting to be free."

"History books are filled with stories of men dying to be free. The men only got it partly right, though," Suzy said.

"How do you mean?" Douglas asked.

"Take for instance my ancestor Alexander Hamilton, on *my father's side, obviously*. He left the Caribbean to be free. Like me and you, he escaped to be free from his horrible childhood too. Then he came here, and still he wasn't free enough; he couldn't abide the British taxing him. No white man could. So he fought against that. He was always fighting to be free. He even fought for the slaves of Washington and Jefferson to be free. He didn't believe our nation could be built on the backs of others, but so many of our founding fathers didn't seem to mind it. As long as *they* were free, then America was *free enough*. They left a lot of others out of the deal— women, slaves, natives. It's a messy business, this search for freedom is," Suzy said, shaking her head.

"The past is always with us. Always holding onto us. Isn't it? In so many ways, we're still fighting the same fights. Trying to undo all the wrongs that our ancestors committed or perpetrated. We are—well, I guess we're just trying to really, truly be free"— she continued—"from our parents, our past, our mistakes, our oppressors." She fell silent for a moment.

Douglas asked, "Do you still feel trapped? By your past? Your mother? Your country? That seemed to be a theme in the book on John Gordon and the Scottish Highlanders—they just wanted freedom. They wanted something better, something more. I think it's universal? Don't you?"

"I think so. I think so many of us suffer because we feel trapped by our past, by expectations, by our own fears. We live in a terror of our own making, and it becomes our reality." Suzy nodded.

"John Gordon did exactly that. In his quest for freedom, he made his life a sort of prison, because no matter how much he had, it was never enough for him. He thought his freedom would be in money and success. Then he thought it would be in his wife and romance. Then he thought it would be in another country—the Colonies. And then he thought it was in a young woman . . ."

Suzy's eyebrows lifted. "So *a scandal* is in your past?"

"Appears to be so. I followed the links from my father's name, and it led to Timothy—the youngest son of John Gordon. Some historians guess that he was a *love child*. Jane wasn't his biological mother, but she raised him as her own. It's ironic because, well, Timothy is a bastard, and so am I . . ."

"What? I thought you said you had a father? I'm confused," Suzy said.

"Don't you have to get back to work?" Douglas hesitated, nervous to share.

"This *is* work! I am helping a client with research," she said, sipping her coffee.

"I don't know if I want to get into it," Douglas said.

"Well, it's not like it happened yesterday, Douglas. It's a different time now. No one is judging you. I'm certainly not," Suzy said.

"Well, I realized something when I was looking through the links, and it's kind of—well—earth-shattering to be honest," Douglas said.

"Wait, you didn't know this up until you started researching?"

"No," Douglas said. "My whole life, right from the beginning, I don't know whether it's all beginning to make total sense— why it was so hard, why we were so isolated, why my father and mother were so—so, so, there is no other word for it, but so *oblivious* to us kids."

"I'm confused, what happened? How are you a bastard like your third great-grandfather Timothy?"

"I found my father on two different census entries. On the first he is married to one woman and has a daughter, and then ten years later, there he is at a nearby address with my mother, older brother, and two sisters. He married the first woman. He then left his first wife and child for his mistress—my mother, whom he had a love child with, my older brother."

"I see." Suzy nodded.

"I mean, my whole life, my father called us his 'little bastards,' and I didn't get it. No one told us this. And he and my mother were lovesick for each other. It was as if we kids didn't exist. I still have memories of being a boy not much older than three, sent to sleep up in an attic, and crying out for my parents and them never coming," Douglas said as he stared out toward the fountain. She could sense that he was deliberately averting his eyes from her. "I know this sounds silly coming from a grown man. But I never felt love. I was never hugged. I was never told, 'I love you.' I felt ashamed, but I didn't know why."

"Oh, Douglas, I am so sorry. That must have been so hard and so scary," Suzy said compassionately.

"It was, but learning this—all of this—it seems to make sense, somehow," Douglas said.

"How so?"

"That maybe it was *genetic*? That my fourth great-grandfather was this romantic fool who had an affair and a bastard child, and my father was destined to repeat the same mistakes. I don't know, but somehow, it feels a bit *better* knowing this. That dreaming and wanting more than what one has is somehow coded into our DNA, and that my father had no choice but to be a hopeless romantic and dreamer."

"But you're not anything like your father. It sounds like you

were a devoted husband, right up until the end. And you didn't
father any children out of wedlock—and you've come a long way
from living in a shack," Suzy reassured him.

"I suppose in some ways I broke free from the past, but in other
ways, not so much," Douglas added.

"You sound like a very loyal person, Douglas. With so much
integrity and purpose. You can own that. Your past doesn't get
to take credit for the good things in your life any more than it's
responsible for all the bad; at the end of the day we're all responsible for our own choices," Suzy said.

"I guess," Douglas agreed tentatively. "But still, I can't get over
the fact that my ancestor was a bastard—like me. Isn't it just, I
don't know, more than a coincidence?"

"Honestly, nowadays the odds are pretty good that it is nothing
more than that," Suzy said.

"I know, but back then, it must have been hard, right? I mean, it
was probably hard for my parents—we never had friendly relationships with many other people. They must have been shunned. Come
to think of it, I may have been as well. Though I was hardly aware
of it as a boy. We didn't think of those things back when we were
kids. But, in the eighteenth century? That couldn't have been easy.
Timothy's brothers, Alexander and William, and his sister Anne;
they had to know, right? It had to cause some sort of strife? There
had to be divisions of loyalty? Wouldn't you think?" Douglas asked.

"I don't know, Douglas, sounds like we need to get you some
books about Timothy and Alexander Macomb, half brothers
during the revolution. Let's go back inside and look them up,"
Suzy suggested.

"I don't think so." Douglas waved her on. "I don't think I can
read anymore. It's too much." Douglas shook his head, feeling his
courage flagging once again.

"But we just got started!"

"*We?*" Douglas asked with a raised eyebrow.

"Yes, 'we,' because now you got me curious. I want to know about the two brothers! I want to know how Alexander became involved with Alexander Hamilton! I want to know how Timothy and Alexander got along and why Alexander fought for the colonies and why Timothy said he sided with the Crown but became a spy," Suzy added. "This is where it gets really interesting."

"It is," Douglas admitted.

"But?" Suzy said.

"But, I didn't realize how much stuff this was going to dredge up for me. I didn't realize I was going to be so—I don't know— pulled back into my own past. I didn't realize how revelatory looking at one's own past can actually be," Douglas said.

"No one ever does," Suzy said. "I've watched so many people like you come to me wanting to find out where they came from— only for them to discover that what matters most to them now, what matters most in their life—is *right now*. Sometimes it takes going back in the past to really understand that," Suzy added.

"And what do you want right now, Suzy?" Douglas asked.

There was a pause, and for the most fleeting moment, Douglas thought he could sense a spark between them. He hadn't meant to imply anything when he'd asked, but now Douglas was wondering what it was that Suzy truly wanted.

"To help you find some books on Timothy and Alexander," Suzy said, breaking the spell in the air by standing up and smoothing out her skirt.

Douglas could see how self-conscious and nervous she had become. He knew she was running away from him, and he wanted to reach out, to reassure her that she could trust him. But he didn't want to act precipitously and scare her away. He knew what he wanted, though. He wanted to see her again and again. He wanted to sit and have another cappuccino with her.

As Suzy turned to head back toward the library entrance, Douglas stood still. He couldn't bring himself to form words. There was so much he wanted to call after her: *Don't go! I want to spend more time with you! It never feels like enough!*

But nothing came out of his mouth, and he watched as Suzy ascended the stairs—getting farther and farther away from him.

When Suzy realized Douglas wasn't behind her, she stopped and looked around, scanning the crowd. Douglas could see in that moment, she wanted him to be near her, too. It wasn't only happening in his imagination. When her eyes locked on his, she waved him up. "Douglas! Aren't you coming back in? We have research to do!"

Douglas nodded and followed Suzy up the stairs, quickly closing the distance between them with every step.

For the rest of the afternoon, Douglas sat in the library and pored over the books that Suzy brought for him. He read about Timothy and Alexander. He read about the fur trade. He read boring texts about the French and Indian War. He didn't care about any of it. He only cared that, across the room, a beautiful woman named Suzy Hamilton was there. They were together. He wasn't alone. There was no past to reconcile. Nothing to fear. Nothing he said to Suzy had scared her away. Nothing he had revealed appeared to make her think any less of him. He didn't have to try to be something he wasn't. He didn't have to worry about feeling anxious or down or depressed. He could just be exactly who he was, and Suzy liked him anyway. These thoughts astounded him. How long had he tried to impress his wife? How long had he worked to make her happy? How long had he feared her disappointment? How long had he suffered over her? Was that love? Was love so one-sided? Had he been wrong to be so devoted to someone who in the end would forget him altogether? Who before she forgot him, had always wanted more? Hadn't he tried to get her to love him? Every patent, every career success and accolade, every home he purchased, it was all for her, and as he would tell everyone, it was because of her. But, was it?

Staring at Suzy from across the wide expanse of the library reading room, he was unsure now. Was love more than devotion? Was love more than lust? Was what he was feeling in the moment—this sense of overwhelming peace and happiness with another human being—*love*? He barely knew the woman. But what he felt stirring inside him, he was sure wasn't *not love*. He felt like he was at home. Only it was a home he had never quite known. Of course, not in his childhood. And no, not even with Hope. How strange life was. How one could share love with cherished others and yet it could feel so different with each person. Was it still love if it felt different? How did one know what love was? How could anyone ever know?

Douglas wrestled with these thoughts all afternoon, which were a welcome distraction from the past, both his ancestors' and his own, but especially his own.

When the library visitors were asked to leave, Douglas stood up and walked over to Suzy at the desk.

"Thank you for the coffee, Suzy, and the conversation. Next time it's on me," Douglas said, pointing to his chest.

"You're on!" she said.

"Wonderful. How about tonight? How much longer till you get off?"

"Oh, Douglas, that's so kind of you, but I have to go see my mother. We have plans," Suzy said.

"Oh, okay. Well, another time then," Douglas said, patting the desk. "Another time."

"Sure, Douglas. Have a good night. And I can't wait to hear all about Timothy and *our* Alexanders," she said.

"Yes, our Alexanders." Douglas nodded. And then boldly, he reached down, took her hand, and kissed it.

4

ALEXANDER MACOMB

Three-times Great-uncle of Douglas McCombs

Born 1748 in Ballyclare, County Antrim, Ireland
Died 1831 in Washington, D.C., United States
Son of John Gordon Macomb and Jane Macomb of Ballyclare,
County Antrim, Ireland,
Brother of William, Anne, and Half Brother of Timothy

April 9, 1792
To William Constable on the occasion of my impending imprisonment

Dearest William,

Oh, how it pains me to write this letter. The shame of it all! I write this grievous letter to impart to you the darkest news and to implore your assistance if not for me, then for my poor wife, Janet, and my children. We have none left to turn to. No, not even my own father.

As you well know by now, despite his failings, my father is a visionary man and has always been so. On the strength of his own ambition, he took my family across the ocean to a strange and uncivilized land. There, he forged a profitable business out of nothing but sheer tenacity and some fortuitous advice. When all hope seemed lost, he proved himself time and time again by rising from the ashes stronger and more successful than before.

He is a man, as I have said before, whose flaws brought him his share of troubles as well. Many do not know this, but my dear mother Jane raised my bastard of a brother, Timothy, as her own to keep my father's lewd, godless affair a secret and, in so doing, preserve his name and that of Timothy, my father's bastard, now known of course as Timothy Macomb. It is for this reason, and for the love of my poor mother now in Heaven, that my father and I have never got on. He and I fell out with one another when I discovered the truth, and I left home shortly thereafter to build a life for my own—free from the lies and faithlessness of my father's house.

It always angered me that my father was protected by my mother's unconditional love, by the strength of her character and her largeness of soul. Neither I nor my mother ever

received love of such quality from my father. He did not deserve to be protected by her then, and yet he was. I am sure if my mother were alive today, she would be here to protect me, too. But, alas, my mother cannot be here for me now unless in spirit, and there is no earthly being to take her place at my side. How the tables have turned! As once I was ashamed of my father, now my father is ashamed of me. I am a Patriot, a traitor to his king, and now also most profoundly in debt. In sum, I am a failure among men in the eyes of John Gordon Macomb. As such I cannot blame him for his cold regard. Much as I did those many years before, he has turned his back on me in this my darkest hour. Now he is lost to me, it seems that there is no one left to whom I may turn but you, dearest friend.

It is likely ill-advised, but still I have hope. I have made a new plan, one which involves both you and our dear mutual friend, Alexander Hamilton.

Now it is true that you may laugh at this, what sounds some visionary scheme to your ears, in the way you always have when in the past I have revealed to you my ambitions. I would not blame you for it. You have counseled me well over the years and always cautioned me to temper my aspirations, not to place too much confidence in my hope for what could be. I am afraid it is of no use—I am an optimiste, you see. Even now I believe all is not lost. Now, as I am writing this very letter you read and preparing myself body and soul to be hauled off to debtors' prison at any moment—now, as my wife prepares to raise all our many children on her own, without even a home to do it in! Even now, I have hope. I believe there is something that you can do, my friend.

But before I make my request, know that I come to you after only the gravest of contemplations, bearing the sincerest apology my soul can muster, and with the promise of a true and *complete accounting to come first and foremost. Please know that I realize the imposition I make upon you, my friend, and the significance of what it is I ask of you. I would not come to you with such a bold request had I not been driven to such a desperate circumstance!*

First: I curse myself for my credulity—for believing in the promises of other men. It is only for the reason that I trusted these aforesaid others to uphold their end of our arrangement that I find myself unable to hold up my own! You have known me for years and have been one of my staunchest friends throughout this life, which has not always been kindest to me. You know it is not in my nature to default on loans or fall back on my word. You must know this. You must know that I have simply found myself in a piteous circumstance, one I will no doubt see my way out of with your most benevolent assistance. This is all merely a moment in time, and in only a moment more I will assuredly find my way again to where I started.

Think back to how fortunate was my situation only a few years ago! The President of the United States, our first, was residing in my mansion on Broadway. The most hallowed residence of our new nation's capital, on my own land. The President entrusted his life and thus the security of our very government to me. I had over twenty-five servants, twelve of them I had no need to pay, being legally bought and purchased.

(Please, William, save your judgments. I have heard them all from our dear friend Alexander Hamilton, who already has nearly convinced me to see the immorality of such practice. I assure you that when I return from prison, I will sign for the release of all twelve.)

Alas, owning slaves and tending a mansion of servants seems of little concern to me now. Hosting President Washington and his consorts for elaborate meals and discussing the future of

our nation seem distant memories now, as if they were nothing more than dreams. Yet in actual fact those events were indeed real and occurred only three short years ago. Look at me now and see the contrast—my credit gone, a large family to support, and myself on my way to prison. Such sad reversal, and all this in the space of fewer than three months!

You may say, as others have, that only I myself am to blame. That I should have been more cautious. The New York City marketplace is a precarious business, and I should have recognized the dangers of speculation in land and securities. Now as we both know, I live in search of opportunity, as my father and all my ancestors before me. I had no way of knowing it would all go so wrong.

And when we speak of wrong, what is it that we mean? Is it wrong to desire more? Is it wrong to dream of lasting fame, to want to be known as the "man who built New York"? This ill-fated purchase of 1792 would have put my family on the map for centuries to come. All that I am truly guilty of is wanting my name to be synonymous with those of our founding fathers, with all the other self-made men of our new republic. Now, granted they were all true Patriots long before we were. You, our friend William Edgar, and I showed our allegiance to our king for far longer than others. How could we be blamed for having prudence in such matters? How ought we have known that the Patriots would be effective fighters? We were protecting our business interests, were we not? As always, were we not opportunists more than we were Loyalists? Above all, we were men of business. There is no greater calling.

Politics be damned! What did politics get my ancestors in Scotland? Slaughtered on the battlefield of Culloden, pushed off their lands, and sent to the far ends of the earth! Much good it did them.

Now, look at you, friend: A trans-Atlantic trader and a most accomplished one at that. When the British won, so did you. When the Patriots won, so also did you win. You played the game well, my boy! You've always been the smarter of the two of us. You kept to the business at hand. Me? I simply could not help myself, could I? Ought I blame my father and my Scottish heritage for wanting more than my fair share of the land? Weren't the Scots always trying to spread their clans over large and still larger tracts of land? Who among us would not desire to be laird of their own castle, head of their own clan? Is that what propels me? Is that what is in me that makes me want more and more? Even more children? Isn't twelve enough? Why, a single child would have been enough! But it would not satisfy me, and I went on to have twelve. I am sure there are more to come! Why not stop at 4.5 million acres of land? Why could I not be satisfied once I had enough? Why did I have to speculate in stocks? What is it inside me that always seems to want more—of everything?

There is word about town that I am what they call a "man on the make." They say that I am a wolf always on the hunt for my next prey. I had never taken it to mean anything negative— let alone anything dangerous or subversive. But, I have begun to see that perhaps I ought to have played the sheep a bit more. Perhaps I would not find myself in such a predicament. Perhaps I should have heeded your wise counsel and not undertaken more than I was able to manage. My ambitions seemed to have simply gotten the better of me.

But had I really any other choice? I was on my own by 1766. I was only eighteen when I struck out for Detroit to become a fur trader. When I was sixteen and my dear mother, God rest her soul, decided to raise my bastard brother Timothy as one of her own, as I have now told you, I could not divest my

conscience of its concern regarding the immorality—the sheer mendacity of it all! I could not abide any longer to sanction my father's disgraced state by virtue of remaining present in his home. I set out on my own to make something of myself on my own terms. Not unlike my father, I suppose I too wanted to be free. I wanted to venture out and see new lands, and the frontier was where I would find adventure and opportunity, but paramount of all, it was the freedom which I sought.

I built myself up from nothing—as you have done, and our dear Alexander. We all did what we had to do to survive. You ran goods for the British, and Alexander ran slave ships out of the Caribbean. Those years we were young and hungry, though we may keep quiet about them in shame, nevertheless they made us strong. They made us want more. We saw life in perfect clarity—stood in the truth of its bleakness and loneliness—and yet strived to make it better.

With no family to support me, I learned to be self-sufficient. I learned that what I did not deign to do myself, no one would. I struggled and scraped, and I made my way to success. No one did that for me! No one did it for you, either. And what have you built? A shipping empire! And by the time that I was only twenty-six years old, I had sponsored my younger brother William to join me. Together we became post agents in Schenectady, and in eleven years' time, we were on the forefront of the war. That's when I met you, of course, my fellow Irish-Scot, and Henry Hamilton, a distant relative of our friend Alexander.

That is the moment when, though I do not purport to be the noblest of men, I am certain that I helped you all. I made no allegiance to country, only a promise to help my friends. I assembled as many Indians as possible to help Henry in the fight for the British. And when you, Alexander, and your Patriots needed supplies, I did as you commanded. I was Henry's chief provisioner through the war. If he or the king wanted for anything, I provided. I did so without requesting commission or expenses. We were more to one another than business partners—we were friends. My fifth son, Henry Hamilton, carries his name. Henry even once wrote a letter on my behalf, asserting that I am a "perfectly honest man." When the British lost the war and he saw I had switched sides for business purposes, he didn't out disown me as a Loyalist. Neither did you and Alexander begrudge me for having been one in the first place. You simply let me be. And yet, you all made me a very wealthy man in the process, which has made it possible for me to move to New York and build a life of abundance as a Patriot, now, of course, and a proper man about town.

Perhaps you more than anyone understood my desire to leave Detroit. I have always enjoyed being on the winning team, have I not? My brother William was always the conservative, of course, and remained behind, loyal to the king to the end. Being content to do the same thing for all of his days with no further ambitions than to be a merchant, to this day he remains in Detroit. I cannot blame him for not sharing my opportunistic vision. He could not possibly have seen the wealth that was possible in New York City under the new, unrestricted freedom of the Patriots. But as for me, I knew I could build my life anew once again. In New York City, no one must know I had ever been a Loyalist in Detroit, or that I might once have helped the Indians purchase their scalping knives—though the telling of that tale still remains between you and me.

Any who did know I was a Loyalist during the war did not seem to mind—our friend Alexander Hamilton among them. He knew it was to his advantage to have some of the old Loyalists on his side—and the money we bring with us. In fact, Alexander used my example to bolster his belief that

political unity was an urgent, national priority. He chose me and my home, my business acumen to help him and his friend, George Washington, spread the message that old Loyalists should be welcomed rather than abhorred. He did not discount me because of my previous alliances. He saw them for what they were: business transactions and nothing more. If there was anything I learned from my father it was what not *to do: Do not impregnate women not your wives, and do not swear any oaths of an allegiance or be politically outspoken, because in the end it will destroy you. Though my father was unfaithful in other ways, he remained loyal to the Crown to his own detriment. I will not follow in his footsteps. I will not die or fall on my sword for a cause I do not believe in. And I do not believe I belong in debtors prison. I do not believe I did anything wrong. I have been generous to a fault, trusting to a fault, and nothing more.*

So by now you must wonder: What is it that I require of you, besides your friendship and loyalty? Aye, now is the time to make my humble request. And I make it of you. There is no one more influential than you. You, my friend, are revered and respected in both Philadelphia and New York. You are a genuine war hero of the great Continental Army. Unlike me, you had the good sense to switch sides just before the war ended and make your name known throughout the land as a Patriot. Well played, indeed!

I also come to you because you, above all others, know my own commitment to New York and our young nation's causes. I have helped with the conversion of the City Hall to the Federal House. I have funded the building of our state archives. I have served as the treasurer of New York's first scientific body, the Society for the Promotion of Agriculture, Arts, and Manufacturers. I am committed.

Finally I come to you because I am also your business partner. As you will recall, both you and Alexander Hamilton also own land in our Ohio Company stock—and in our secret purchase upstate that made us the majority landowners of New York. Some have gone so far as to call our purchase collusion, and to accuse me—or should I say us?—of bribing Governor Clinton to make the vast purchase. Of course, I would never accuse a friend of mine, especially you, of such a heinous crime. And to prove it, at your request I even kept your name a secret in the great purchase—to protect yours and Alexander's identity. I see that I looked as though I was a sole bidder of this supposed great purchase, incurring onerous debt that my sentence to debtors prison is intended to collect on. Now I know you, a noble, good, and loyal friend would not have kept your name secret if you thought it were possible I alone would take the fall when political adversaries came looking for someone to imprison. No, that thought would never cross my mind.

Why, if it had been the case that you and Alexander had, in fact, wanted me to take the fall, Alexander would never have named me to the board of the Bank of the United States, his grand idea to federalize our nation's banks. And he would never have made that secret agreement this past December—our one-year program of speculation in bank stocks. Why would he have arranged it such that all the decisions lay in our friend Duer's control, but all the paperwork stood in my name only? If I am guilty of anything, it is this: Trusting someone else to make decisions in my name—risking all that I own, most importantly, my good name.

Aye, you warned me of this folly. You left for London, and by the time I got your letter warning that Duer would speculate using my good name and reap all the profit for himself, while I would pocket the loss, it was too late. The warning didn't arrive in time. Your predictions were true and correct.

Our speculation failed. Worst of all, I had committed all of my assets—including my beloved home. As you know, my beloved wife, Mary Catherine, and I once dreamed we would raise all of our children there. We had hoped it would be a place of gathering and joy, the repository of all of our life's work. Now I cannot bear to bring myself to so much as step foot in the place. The memory of our lost hopes and dreams are still too fresh and painful. Even though I have found support and love with my wife Janet, I can't help but feel a loyalty to Mary Catherine. I can feel her disappointment in me from beyond the grave. I can only imagine the shame she would have felt, were she still alive. It is a blessing she did not live to see my fall from grace. I gambled our home—our children's home. What have I done? But truth be told, even if I didn't lose the house in this folly, I still don't think I could ever bring myself to go back there for fear of meeting her ghost. What would she think of me?

Look at me now: I am bankrupt. Marauders and note-holders hunt me down day and night and will give me not a moment's peace. I could not return home if I wanted to—they loiter about my home, hoping to see me. I am a marked man. As if my life were not enough, they will also have everything I do not have to give as well! I owe nearly $300,000 and have no idea how to procure such a staggering amount in my present circumstances. I know you too are facing your own financial troubles. I do not come to you for money. Rather, I come for intervention. Surely, you can ask our friend Alexander to step in on my behalf? After all, he alone knows what Duer did. He was there when we signed the contract. He knows that Duer did the speculating with my

*good name! He knows also all that I have given for our coun-
try without reward—I have purchased all the land that he
holds in his name. I gave my home to be used by the President!
I built many buildings in New York, and I have given my life
in service to so many Patriot causes. Can these acts not count
for something? If my successes have not been enough to count
for something, perhaps Alexander can see my failures as great
lessons for our new country? We have created such things as
corporations and consortiums—federal banks and stocks. We
have paved the way for businessmen and countrymen for centuries. Our loss shall be the gain of men of the future!*

*William, please, I have no one else to turn to. I have many
young children, a new wife who is expecting yet another child,
and I am all alone in this world. All I have left is my friend-
ships—yours and Alexander's the best of them. The both of
you are my last and only good hope. He is not answering my
letters. He is apparently embroiled in an urgent affair of his
own—some unseemly business with a mistress whose husband
requires payment to keep quiet. I suppose we all have our share
of troubles these days.*

*I wish you well, my friend. I wouldn't wish this horrible sit-
uation on anyone—not even an enemy. I pray for your answer
to my letter soon. You and Alexander are all my wife and I
have now.*

Yours in gratitude and friendship,

Alexander Macomb

5

WELL, TONIGHT
WE'LL CHANGE THAT

*D*ouglas had made all the arrangements for his first date with Suzy. He secured a reservation at Eleven Madison Park, which was rated as the Zagat's "best restaurant in the world." *A ranking like this is only fitting for Suzy,* he thought. He wanted to show her how much he appreciated her friendship, and just any restaurant wouldn't do.

Ever since she had accepted his invitation, Douglas could think of nothing else. For the past few days he could do little more than replay their interactions over and over in his mind.

Just days earlier, he had returned a book on the life of Alexander Macomb to her at the library. He had no intention of asking her out. He was simply going to return the book and leave. He was, after all, trying hard not to overplay his hand. But he couldn't believe what had come over him. It was as if a new, emboldened, risk-taking version of himself had replaced his old self. Before Suzy even had a chance to say hello, it was out of his mouth already. "Would you like to join me for dinner this Friday?"

Suzy didn't hesitate, which is what Douglas remembered most. The way she'd immediately said, "I'd love to!" without even thinking about it—as if she had been waiting for him to ask.

It was all the confirmation he needed. She was as excited about going out with him as he was with her. Suzy even wrote down her address and slid it to him so he could pick her up.

But just as Douglas was turning to go, Suzy called out to stop him. For a split second, Douglas hesitated to turn around. *What if she changed her mind?* he wondered. Douglas turned slowly and looked up at her.

"What should I wear?"

Relief washed through this entire body. He didn't realize how much he had tensed up in that brief but excruciating moment.

"Anything! You'll look beautiful no matter what," Douglas boldly said, now regaining his confidence again.

"Thank you, Douglas, you're so sweet," Suzy said. "But should I wear a dress or jeans or something in between?"

"I'm going to take you somewhere nice, but I wouldn't presume to tell you how to dress."

Suzy nodded as a smile spread across her face. Douglas could tell she liked that answer.

"What time?" Suzy asked.

"Oh, right. I didn't give you a time. I'll swing by around seven p.m.," Douglas said.

"Perfect! I'll look forward to it!"

Douglas walked out of the library with a new sense of purpose. He began researching restaurants and making calls as soon as he returned home.

Douglas hadn't taken a woman out to dinner in years. He wanted to make sure it was a good one—and one that didn't stir up any memories. He couldn't take her to any of the places he had been with Hope. No, he didn't want to spend the night remembering or comparing. This was all going to be new—and he was ready for *new*. He was ready for excitement, joy, and feeling young again. Though he never admitted it to anyone else, he was also looking forward to the possibility of romance, desire, and sex. It had been years since he had been intimate with his wife. He had lived for years like a live-in nurse. He had often been so exhausted by the end of each day that he didn't desire anyone at all. In fact, he didn't think it would be possible for him to ever be with a woman again. When he was in Thailand on business years ago, someone wanted to arrange to have a woman sent to him as a "token of appreciation." The mere thought of hiring a prostitute repulsed him. No matter how lonely and undesired he felt, he would never resort to such a thing. Since that moment, he thought for sure his days as a sexual being were over. Since it was unthinkable for him to hire someone, then he had no other options. He certainly couldn't imagine meeting someone he might love ever again.

But Suzy had stirred something in him. He not only felt desirous of her—*he felt desired*. He couldn't even remember the last time he felt desired—if at all. He loved his wife, but he had been the pursuer throughout their entire marriage. He had met her as a girl. They were mere children then, and they approached their young married life as children. She liked to be fawned over, taken care of, and protected. She had always been taken care of by her own parents, and when she married him she had expected him to do the same. From the beginning of their relationship, in order to show just how much he loved her, he did everything possible to make her happy—even if it made him unhappy in the process. He thought that was what love was.

He thought true love meant giving everything one had to someone else—even if they couldn't give back in equal measure. So that's what he did. He gave like a father does to his children— without expectation or reciprocation. He gave it unconditionally and wholeheartedly. If she wanted something, he gave it to her. In so many ways, he had become her caretaker long before Alzheimer's had in effect taken her away from him. Throughout their entire married life, he parented her. In many ways, she was the child they never had. Before they had married she had said she wanted children, but as soon as she had the ring on her finger, it all became too real for her. She didn't want to grow up, have the responsibility, and so she came to him and put it quite plainly.

"I don't want children, Douglas. Ever."

Though Douglas had tried to cajole her by "coming at her sideways," as he used to call his tactical approach to getting her to try new things, she simply said "no" every time he asked or brought it up. If Hope didn't want children, he figured, he would eventually learn not to want children too. But he never did. The desire for them remained. Just as his desire for her remained, unrequited so often as it was. She didn't want to try new things, explore, be adventurous, or even have fun.

"Stop behaving that way, Douglas. You'll embarrass yourself," she would say to him whenever he tried to get her to lighten up and try something new. After awhile, he just stopped trying all together. He had shut down that part of himself so long ago, that now he didn't know it even existed within him—until a few weeks ago when Suzy walked into his life. He wondered what else could change. *What else had he been missing out on all those years?*

. . .

Just before picking Suzy up, Douglas called Mark to let him know what he had planned for the evening.

"That's terrific, Douglas! Really!"

"You don't think it's too soon? Or that . . . I shouldn't be dating at my age?" Douglas wondered.

"Nonsense, Douglas! This is exactly what you need! You're still alive! You've got so much to live for and so much love in you left to give. This is the best news I've heard in a long time. In fact, it's the happiest I've heard you sound in a long time!"

"I *am* happy," Douglas responded, as if it was some sort of revelation he hadn't consciously acknowledged until it was confirmed by Mark. "I do feel good. I think Suzy is terrific. We have so much to talk about when we're together."

"Dinner together will be a great start then! Where are you taking her?"

"Eleven Madison Park," Douglas said with smile.

"Ah! You're pulling out the big guns for this one! I like it. I am sure she'll love it too. Are you picking her up?"

"I am. She gave me her address and everything."

"Will you bring her flowers?"

"Do people still do that? I haven't been on a first date in nearly fifty years. I was a teenager when I picked up Hope on our first date—and I had to meet her father!"

"I think flowers are always a nice gesture. I say go for it."

"Are *you sure* you don't think I am being foolish? Dating at my age?"

"Absolutely not! I've said it before and I'll say it again: Douglas, you're still alive. Do you hear me, Douglas? You're *alive*. That's all that matters right now, and there is absolutely nothing wrong in doing things that make you happy and make you feel whole inside."

"Then why do I feel so guilty? Why do I feel so ashamed?" Douglas asked quietly.

"I think it's natural. I think it's because you're a good person and you spent your entire life *living* for Hope. You don't know how to do something for yourself. You don't know how to feel joy. It's been a long time. It's going to take some time. It's not going to happen overnight. But, it can happen moment by moment. Date by date. Just see where this night takes you. That's all you have to do. You deserve this joy, Douglas. You do. No one will judge you for it. Just because you're happy now doesn't mean you love Hope any less. Do you understand?"

"I do." Douglas nodded. "Thank you for understanding."

"I don't want you to be late. You better get going!" Mark said. "And pick up some flowers!"

"Okay!"

"And call me tomorrow. I'll want to hear how it all went."

"I will! I'm off! Wish me luck!"

"You don't need luck, Douglas. You've got this!"

• • •

Mark was right: The flowers were a hit. When Suzy opened her apartment door to see Douglas standing there with them, her entire face lit up.

"You brought me flowers! How lovely! Come in, come in!" Suzy opened wide the door and waved him over the threshold.

"I'll put these in water and then we can get on our way," Suzy said, walking toward the kitchen.

"No rush, we have time. Reservations aren't until eight p.m. I didn't know how traffic would be, but we're in good shape to make it on time," Douglas said as he took in Suzy's small but carefully appointed apartment. She was neat, eclectic, and by the looks of all the books on shelves, tables, and every available surface, she was every bit as well read as he expected a librarian to be.

As Suzy came out of the kitchen with the vase filled with roses, she said, "Oh, Douglas, they're beautiful!"

Douglas turned to look at the roses but could only see Suzy—she was wearing tall heels and a little black dress. He inhaled deeply, feeling suddenly flushed and overwhelmed by the mere sight of her.

"Wow!"

"Yes, they're gorgeous," Suzy said, fussing over the roses as she placed them on her dining room table.

"No, I meant *you*. Wow. You look amazing."

"Oh, Douglas!" she said shyly. "Did I do too much? Am I overdressed?"

"No! You're perfect!"

"We'll, I'll just grab my shawl and we can go."

Suzy walked quickly down the hall and disappeared into her bedroom and came out wearing a brightly colored scarf draped over her shoulders.

When they reached the sidewalk, Douglas took Suzy's hand, and a deep breath that he tried to conceal, and said, "Shall we?" and led her to the car.

"You hired a car and driver? We're not walking? Where are we going?"

"It's a surprise." Douglas winked as the driver opened the car door for her.

When the car arrived at Eleven Madison Park, Suzy looked out the window and balked.

"No way," she said.

"What? You don't like it?"

Suzy turned and shook her head. "It's just that . . . no one has ever . . ." She stopped speaking and shook her head.

"Did I do something wrong? Does this place bring up bad memories? I tried to go for something fairly new. It's an older restaurant, but it was just renovated . . ."

"No! It's perfect. There's absolutely nothing wrong with the restaurant. It's me, Douglas."

"*You?* What's wrong with you?" Douglas said, surprised that Suzy would be nervous or self-conscious. He thought he was the only one who ever felt that way.

"I'm fifty years old, Douglas, and this is the first time a man has ever treated me so kindly—flowers, a car, and now this—it's too much!"

"Nonsense! You deserve some joy and happiness. A good friend just had to tell me the same thing, and you're no exception! Now, let's go and have some fun—and a world-class meal—shall we?" Douglas said, getting out of the car and running around the back to open the door for Suzy.

Suzy nodded and said nothing but turned and took one more look at the entrance.

"So you've heard of this place?" Douglas asked.

"I have. I read the restaurant reviews in the *Times* every week. I've just never been to a restaurant that's been reviewed."

"Well, tonight we'll change that," Douglas said, leaning over and taking her hand in his.

• • •

They sat and talked for hours. The courses were served. The plates came and went, but for all the world, Douglas and Suzy didn't notice the food at all. They were lost now, as those on first dates usually are, in each other's eyes, in their stories, in their pasts.

"Do you always eat in such fancy places?" Suzy asked as one plate was removed and another placed in front of her.

"No. Well, not lately," Douglas said. "I order in mostly. But, I used to. Hope and I—"

"Your wife?" Suzy interjected

"Yes, Hope and I used to travel and eat out quite a bit before she got sick. She liked the finer things. In fact, nothing was too good for her."

"I see," Suzy said. "And you miss it? The traveling and eating out?"

"I do," Douglas admitted. "I've always enjoyed it. Though, truth be told, my wife didn't love it as much as I did—at first."

"No? Why?"

"She was a different type of person. It's hard to explain."

"Try, I want to know—everything," Suzy said, urging Douglas to talk.

"Well, we met when we were teenagers. I was poor. Her father didn't think much of me. I had to prove myself worthy of her. And she was accustomed to a different way of life. She was doted on by her parents. I didn't have that sort of childhood."

"I see." Suzy nodded.

"So after we were first married, I worked in research. I was getting a bit too popular for her liking—and had to be away a lot. I couldn't always be there to take care of her. She didn't like that. She wouldn't let me travel. She hated being alone. She was always used to being with her parents or with me."

"What did you end up doing?"

"Well, if I absolutely had to go—she stayed with her parents or friends. But eventually, it began to strain our relationship, so I just quit my job."

"You quit because your wife didn't want you to travel?" Suzy asked incredulously.

"I did. She wanted me to work with her father. He ran a meat-packing business. So I did that for a time."

"You're a good man," Suzy said. "You gave up your life as an inventor and researcher for your wife! I can't imagine asking someone to do such a thing."

"Well, when you put it like that, I guess I didn't look at it that way at the time. And no, I eventually went back to inventing, but on my own terms. I think in the end it turned out to be a good thing. I wouldn't have known I had a knack for business if I didn't get a taste for it while in meat-packing. Eventually, I used those business and managing skills when I started to build my own business, patenting my own inventions and so on. Everything I have in my life I owe to Hope," Douglas said flatly.

"Hmph," Suzy responded, sipping her water.

"What's that supposed to mean?" Douglas asked.

"I don't really know," Suzy said. "It's just you talk very highly of someone you lived for and did everything for. Seems to me that you succeeded in spite of her, not *because* of her. You give her too much credit."

"I don't know about that," Douglas said.

"I do," Suzy said emphatically.

"If it weren't for her I wouldn't have taken so many risks."

"Why do you say that?"

"When I was a boy, I didn't have much. I told you about all that," Douglas said. "I never felt secure or safe. I was always looking for security. Always looking for a solid foundation, I had to work from a young age. It made me hungry for security. Hope was my secure foundation. Hope and I created a life that was grounded. We never moved. We lived in our first home our entire lives. Even after I achieved financial security, we never felt the need to move. She kept me grounded. With her I became much stronger, more confident. And because of that I could take risks where it counted. I could invest in myself."

"Your parents and Hope must have been so proud of you then?"

"Not exactly. My parents weren't very involved in my life—from the beginning."

"Why was that?"

"I think I told you what I discovered about my father and mother when I was doing the research."

"Yes, that your father had a wife and a daughter before he met your mother. That he never married your mother."

"Yes, exactly. My mother and father had a love affair, and I was a result of that. At first it made me angry. I was furious, actually. But then the more I thought about it, the more I realized that my father loved my mother, and he stayed with her. They raised four children together. He may have deserted his wife and daughter, but he didn't desert my mother and his four bastards. I always thought our family was just one more of my father's many failures. But now that I am thinking about it, I see it as one of his achievements. *He stayed.* Given all the failures and poverty and turmoil, he stayed. He could have walked away. I never thought of him as a man with any strength of character. He didn't hold a job or follow through on anything, but the one thing he did manage to do well in his life was love my mother. That counts for something, doesn't it?"

"I think it does," Suzy said. "I had a father who didn't stay, who didn't have the gumption. So I think it does stand for something."

"Do you blame your father for leaving?"

"I think you get to a certain point in life and you have stop blaming others—especially your parents—for the way you turn out in life. Eventually, everyone has to take responsibility for their own actions."

"I totally agree." Douglas nodded. "In fact, I would take it a step further and say I am grateful for my father's missteps and failings as a father."

"Grateful? How so?"

"Well, my father kept me from going to college. It turned out for the best. I ended up working my way through on my own. I valued my education that much more. And the fact that I worked so much as a young boy didn't hurt me either," Douglas explained. "I learned what it was like to work. I appreciate the labors of men and women. I was a better employer because of that. I have been hungry and I have been deprived. I see that in others and I want them to succeed. It's made me a better leader," Douglas added.

"That's noble. Not everyone turns out that way. Poverty and suffering affects everyone differently. Some people become horribly greedy, because they want more and more to feel secure. Some people seem to take their anger and troubles out on the world. You didn't do either, it seems to me," Suzy said.

"No, what I did was I accumulated skill sets to be more secure. I always had a way to make a living, because I could do something of value. I learned one skill set and then another and another. I built a pyramid of security out of skills. I invested in myself."

"Like your ancestors invested in land," Suzy said.

"Yes, something like that. *I* was the commodity, not the land. It was me that I was adding to."

"I guess it runs in your family tree. I read that book you brought back on Monday—about your ancestor Alexander Macomb," Suzy revealed.

"You did? Why?"

"I did. Because I was curious, and to be honest, I thought if the conversation was boring or we ran out of things to talk about, at least we would have something in common to discuss."

Douglas looked at his watch. "So, I guess if you're bringing up the book now—three hours in—we haven't done half bad in the conversation department?" He smiled.

"Oh, no! That's not why I am bringing him up now! We truly haven't run out of things to say. It's just that, I couldn't help but notice—well, how similar you are to your ancestors."

"Similar? I am nothing like Alexander Macomb!"

"Really?" Suzy laughed. "Not even a little?"

"What do you mean? He was a risk-taker—a gambler!"

"He was an innovator!" Suzy argued. "He invested in land, the way you invested in yourself. You both saw potential when no one else did!"

"Okay, so we were both entrepreneurs. But I think that is where the similarities end."

"I don't think so!" Suzy argued again with a grin. "Did you read that letter to Constable in the book?"

"I did. In fact, that excerpt stood out," Douglas acknowledged.

"He couldn't bring himself to go back to the home that he built with his wife. He was devoted to his wife, even after her death. Even if he hadn't lost the house in bankruptcy, he said he would never be able to go back . . . now doesn't that sound familiar? You yourself said, you haven't been back home in years."

"Okay, I see your point."

"He was also incredibly generous and loyal—to a fault. He trusted his friends, and they took advantage of him."

"No one has taken advantage of me!" Douglas argued.

"I'm not saying just *anyone* has—but I think Hope definitely benefited from your blind faith and unwavering loyalty, that is for sure. All I am saying is Alexander Macomb and you do have a lot of similarities. And you were both friends with Hamiltons!"

"Yes, we are! I did find that fascinating," Douglas acknowledged.

"Did you know Hamilton did come to his aid?"

"He did? How did you find that out?"

"Well, I did some digging. I found an article in *The Wall Street Journal* of all places. In 1997 they did a story on the first Wall Street Panic. It was about how William Duer's speculations ultimately resulted in his collapse. It looks like Duer then reached out to his friend Alexander Hamilton for help. But Hamilton didn't respond to him. I think Hamilton was trying to distance himself from the man who used his other friend's name to make such risky wagers. Duer never recovered. But in the article it says that Macomb's name was eventually restored."

"So you think Alexander interceded on my uncle's behalf instead of Duer's?"

"I do," Suzy said, nodding. "He had all the power. He was secretary of the treasury. He would have been the only one with the influence and power to act on Macomb's behalf. I also think Hamilton didn't want to be accused of what we call insider trading today—by using or disseminating Duer's tips. I think he eventually saw Duer for the scoundrel he was and your uncle for the more honorable man he was."

"Hmmm. Interesting."

"What?"

"It's just, you're right. I have more in common with my ancestor than I originally thought. The idea of restoring one's name, I get that."

"Why?"

"I was so ashamed of my own name growing up."

"How come?"

"My older brother was a criminal. He spent some time in jail. He stole cars, broke into places, got into fights. I didn't want anything to do with him," Douglas explained. "He tortured me as a kid. He made my life miserable. He used to try to suffocate me with pillows! I was claustrophobic for years because of it."

"Wow, I am so sorry to hear that. He sounds awful, Douglas."

"He was. He made my life hell. And when he got older—and bigger—I finally fought back, so he stopped getting violent with me. But he still managed to screw up my life," Douglas said, shaking his head at the memory.

"Why? What did he do to you?"

"It wasn't so much *him*, but the cops. Because my name was McCombs, they thought I was bad news too, like my brother. And Hope's ex-boyfriend, Harry, had a brother who was a cop. He didn't like me at all. He blamed me for Hope ending things with Harry. When I was old enough to drive, he went out of his way to follow me around and pull me over for no reason. I wished for all the world to get away from him. Make my own path," Douglas said.

"Again, you're like your ancestors. Didn't Alexander Macomb want to get away from his half brother? Your direct ancestor—Timothy? Seems brotherly love isn't a Macomb family value." Suzy laughed.

"You're right. I didn't think of that connection, either. We don't get to pick our family—or our name. We're stuck with them until we can grow up and move on. Alexander did just that. And, I guess, so did I. Though I do wonder what happened to Timothy. Nothing is written about him. He seems to vanish. Maybe, who knows, maybe Timothy felt like me too," Douglas wondered.

"Felt like what?"

"I just wanted to be someone else. I was always so ashamed. I bet Timothy felt shame too. I wonder if it was difficult living under the shadow of his brother. All I wanted when I was young was to feel proud of who I was," Douglas said.

"And do you feel proud now—now that you know so much about your storied past? Does it make you feel better about sharing a name with your brother?" Suzy asked.

"I suppose it does. It doesn't take away the painful memories, but yes, knowing that my name is so much bigger than me, bigger than my brother—knowing the sacrifices others made, the genius of my ancestors—does help take out the sting of it," Douglas said.

"That must be a nice feeling," Suzy said, absently looking straight ahead, suddenly trying to avoid eye contact with Douglas.

"What do you mean, 'must be a nice feeling'?" Douglas wondered.

"You have an advantage in your healing process, an advantage most people will never get," Suzy said flatly.

"Oh? And what's that?"

"Well, you *know* where you come from. You know your past.

And you have people who, I don't know, sort of help redeem you. You know about them and their motives. I'll never know where my ancestors came from, truly. Well, at least half—the black half, that is. The Hamilton history is well known, and yes, I checked, my line descends from Alexander Hamilton's line. But I'll never know the extent or origin of my mother's side," Suzy said.

"Why?" Douglas asked.

"Why?" Suzy exclaimed, clearly shocked by the very question. "Because she descends from slaves, Douglas! At some point, the journey to the past ends. Their names are lost. Their stories are too. Don't you wonder who were Macomb's slaves? Where did they go after he lost his home? No one ever thinks about the unnamed people in history. And it's not just the slaves or Native Americans. It's the women too. They're all lost to history. I wonder about his wife—Janet—the one who was alive. I wonder how difficult it must have been for her to endure such a scandal and have to figure out how to care for and raise so many children, half of them who weren't even her own, all the while managing her husband's ego and despair over the loss of his fortune—not to mention his previous beloved wife. None of that could have been easy."

"You're right. We don't really know much about women and slaves—all the people who really built our nation."

"No, we don't. We only hear about who wrote the history—white men."

"Does that upset you? Anger you?" Douglas asked. "Does doing this type of research for me, anger you?"

"Anger me? No. It doesn't anger me." Suzy let out a short laugh. "I just like pointing out the questions most people don't think to ask. I like to investigate the silent players in history, the ones no one pays attention to. To me, that's what's really interesting. That's how we get the full story of how we came to be. Over the years, I have helped a lot of people like you. They come to me and ask: 'Can you help me find so-and-so?' And I say yes, and then I ask them why they want to find this person or persons. And they invariably say something to the effect of, 'I want to know where I came from and why I am the way I am.'"

Douglas bowed his head and blushed. He had said as much when he first came to her, even if he had been drawn to her for a totally different reason.

"Don't be embarrassed, Douglas! I am not making fun of you. I am not. I am just telling you what I know and what I have seen and what I think about it."

"And what do you think about all of this? Do you think there is any point in discovering these things? In wondering?"

"Of course I do. But I am not naïve. And what I like about you is that you're not either. You get it. You don't blame your parents for who you are. You don't even blame your wife—in fact, you give her credit! Perhaps more than she deserves, if you ask me. You asked me if the quest is worth it. If there is any point in finding out about one's past. Does it add anything? And my answer is yes. It does. It helps because *we start asking questions—the really important questions*. We start seeing there are even more questions and unknowns than we ever imagined. We start to see that there are so many more people who are responsible for who we become—more than just one white man from long ago. When we start to dig into our pasts, we discover we're a combination of where we came from, who we grew up with, who we worked with, who raised us, and all the people who came before us—uncles, great-great uncles, wives, slaves, grandparents, great-grandparents, and friends of great-grandparents, and on and on. On this whole earth there is no one person quite like us. But at the same time we carry some of the characteristics of each of those who have gone before us."

"Wow, I'm impressed," Douglas said with a smile. "You're so wise."

"I don't know about that," Suzy said demurely. "I am just a librarian."

"No, that's one of the most brilliant things I have ever heard a person say. You're so intelligent, straightforward, and courageous. You have a courage and honesty in you that I've never seen. It's remarkable," Douglas said, astonished.

"You are courageous too, Douglas!" Suzy replied. "You have the same courage Alexander Macomb did. You have his loyalty and heart, too. And there is so much more to find out."

"Yes, there is," Douglas agreed.

"Where to next?" Suzy said.

"How about a walk?"

Suzy let out a loud laugh. "I meant, where to next in our search for our past?"

"There will be plenty of time to talk about the past," Douglas said, lifting his napkin from his lap and raising a finger to call for the check. "But, for now, I'd like to stay fully present. Right here in this moment is the only place I want to be"—he paused—"if that's okay with you."

"Yes, that's fine with me," Suzy said, reaching out and squeezing Douglas's hand. "Absolutely fine."

• • •

When the driver arrived, Douglas gave the address, "39 Broadway, please."

"I thought we were going for a walk?"

"We will. When we get downtown."

"Where are you taking me now?"

"It's another surprise."

When they arrived at 39 Broadway, Douglas opened the car door and took Suzy's hand. "I want to show you something."

"You're taking me to a Duane Reade," Suzy said, looking up in puzzlement.

"No, no, no," Douglas laughed, and then he pointed to a small nondescript bronze bas-relief plaque near the door of 39 Broadway.

"The McComb Mansion, Site of Second Presidential Mansion occupied by General George Washington, February 23 to August 30, 1790. This tablet placed by Colonial Chapter Daughters of the Revolution 1939," Suzy read aloud. "Wow."

"Yep, this is all that's left. That stately four-story mansion fit for a king—or should I say the duly-elected president of a democracy. It's now a plaque next to a Duane Reade," Douglas said. "So much for history leaving its mark."

"You can't say that. History is more than a plaque. And besides, it's still *something*. Your family's name is on a plaque with George Washington. All the slaves that lived and worked in that house will never have their name on a plaque," Suzy commented.

"Point taken," Douglas remarked, staring at the plaque. "It just makes you wonder. What do we leave behind? What's it all add up to? All the work, the success, the love?"

"It adds up to a life, Douglas," she said. "Most of us don't even get a plaque, let alone rewards in life. You can't live your life waiting for someone else to remember you or congratulate you. If you do, you'll be waiting a long time." Suzy was still staring at the plaque, avoiding eye contact.

Douglas turned to look at her. She was so direct. So honest. So intelligent. It excited him in every way. He never in his life had experienced this feeling. What the feeling was exactly, he couldn't explain. His chest felt as though it was expanding from the inside. His mind was racing. There was so much he wanted to say, to know, to learn. There was so much he wanted to know about her. She didn't care what others thought of her. She didn't live her life waiting for—or even expecting—rewards or accolades. She clearly didn't need to be taken care of. She was so easy to talk to and up for any kind of adventure. Here she was standing in front of him, challenging him. Talking to him as an equal. She was a woman in every sense of the word. How had he lived his whole life without this experience?

"How?" Douglas muttered.

Suzy turned and looked at him quizzically. "What? What do you mean by 'how'?"

"I am sorry. I was thinking: How did I get here?"

"Like when you were at the White House getting your award?" Suzy asked and laughed.

"No! How did I get here with you—a person like you? And how did you get to be the person you are? So strong, opinionated, intelligent—it's just, I don't know—so exhilarating."

"Oh, Douglas," she said, shaking her head and walking.

"Are you leaving?" Douglas asked worriedly.

"No! I'm walking. You promised me a walk. Let's go," she said, moving quickly ahead of him.

Douglas quickened his step to match her short, brisk, and utterly confident stride.

"Did I just come on too strong? Did I make you nervous? I am sorry. I am new to this. It's been years since I've been on a date," Douglas explained.

"No, Douglas. Not at all. I find your honesty refreshing. And you're not the only one who is nervous. Believe me," she said.

"So what is your story? I've been talking so much about me and Hope, I don't know anything about you. Were you married?"

"I was. A long time ago. I was young and it was not a good match. Let's just leave it at that," she said quietly.

"Let's not—just leave it at that. Why did it end? I told you my story. I want to hear yours," Douglas asked.

"Well, if you must know, it ended because we had no business starting it in the first place. I had a controlling and dominating mother—so the first guy that came along with the promise to get me away from her, I married. He was an escape route—or so I thought. But, you know that old saying—'out of the frying pan into the fire'? I went from a bad situation to a worse one. I thought my mother was controlling! Huh! He made living with her look like a holiday. I lost all my freedom. And eventually my will to live," she said honestly.

Douglas looked at her out of the side of his eyes and stopped. "You? I can't imagine you being . . . I don't know, depressed? You're so lively and happy!"

"Well, I am now. I am not married to him anymore! But, it took me years to get my wits back. Eventually, I went to school, got my degree in library science. I got my own apartment. And I learned day by day how to be happy."

"And how does one learn how to be happy?" Douglas inquired.

"You start by living in the moment—taking one moment at a time. When you do that, there is no past to remember, no regrets, no pain. And there is no future to stress about. There is only right here and right now. It could be a cup of coffee. It could be enjoying a great book. It could be taking a walk and talking with a person. It's living in the here and now, every day and all day. And then it's lying in bed at night and replaying only the good moments, the ones you're grateful for—the good people that came in and made your day a little better or the people you helped along their way. It all adds up. I did that every day and then every year, and before I knew it, I woke up one day and realized: I'm happy. I'm just happy. I loved my life. I loved every bit of it. I loved my apartment, my job, my friends. And then someone walked into the library one day and wanted to know about his past, and I thought, *I can do that. I can help him*. And that feeling—that you can help someone and make them happy—that's the most wonderful feeling in the world," she said, turning and looking up at Douglas.

He stopped and took Suzy's hands in his. Her eyes lit up as a broad and lovely smile spread across her face. He wanted to take her face in his hands and kiss her. He wanted to wrap his arms around her and never let her go. He wanted to be with her in every moment of her happiness. He didn't need a plaque on a wall. He didn't need an award. He just needed Suzy.

"You are a light, Suzy Hamilton. Pure light," Douglas said.

Instead of taking her face in her hands and kissing her, he squeezed her hands tightly and then let them go. *There would be time for a kiss later*, he thought. Right now, he was going to take Suzy's advice. He was going to live here in this moment—with her. He would take her small hand in his and walk all the way up Broadway and let the world around them fall away. There would be no past. The McComb Mansion plaque would disappear far behind them, and the unknown future would be far out ahead of them—no trouble to them now. Yes, Douglas would live in this moment, in this present, with Suzy, and he would be happy.

6

John McCombs
and
Alexander Macomb, Jr.

John McCombs

Two-times Great-grandfather of Douglas McCombs

Born April 26, 1792, in Old Bennington County, Vermont
Died Sept 21, 1865, in Grantham, St. Catharines, Niagara
Regional Municipality, Ontario, Canada
Son of Timothy Macomb (Half Brother of Alexander Macomb Sr.)
and Sarah Macomb
Cousin of Alexander Macomb Jr.
Grandson of John Gordon Macomb and Jane Macomb
of Ballyclare, County Antrim, Ireland

Major General Alexander Macomb, Jr.,
2nd Commanding General of the United States Army
Awarded Congressional Medal of Honor

Two-times Great-uncle of Douglas McCombs

———

Born April 3, 1782, in Detroit, Michigan
Died June 25, 1841, in Washington, D.C., United States
Son of Alexander Macomb and Mary Catherine Navarre,
Grandson of John Gordon Macomb and Jane Macomb
of Ballyclare, County Antrim, Ireland,

Letter to the Honorable Sec. of War on the Occasion of the Battle of Plattsburgh

Fort Moreau, Sept. 12, 1814

Sir, I have the honor to inform you that the British army, consisting of four brigades, a corps of artillery, a squadron of horse, and a strong light corps, amounting, in all, to about fourteen thousand men, after investing this place, on the north of Saranac river, since the 5th inst. broke up their camp, and raised the siege this morning, at 2 o'clock; they are now retreating precipitately, leaving their sick and wounded behind. The enemy opened his batteries yesterday morning, and continued the cannonading, bombarding, and rocket-firing, until sunset; by this time our batteries had completely silenced those of our opponents.

The light troops, and militia, are now in full pursuit of the enemy, making prisoners in all directions; deserters are continually coming in, so that the loss of the British army, in this enterprise, will be considerable.

A more detailed report will be made of the siege, and circumstances attending it, as soon as possible.

The officers, and men, have all done their duty. The artillery, and the engineers, have performed their functions, with a zeal and precision highly creditable to themselves, and honorable to their country. Our loss is trifling, indeed; having only 1 officer and 15 men killed, and 1 officer and 30 men wounded.

The militia of New-York, and volunteers of Vermont, have been exceedingly serviceable, and have evinced a degree of patriotism, and bravery, worthy of themselves and the states to

which they respectively belong. The strength of the garrison is only 1,500 effective men, rank and file.

> *I have the honor, &c.*
> *Alex Macomb*
> *Hon. Sec. War.*

In our national gallery of distinguished men, the portrait of Alexander Macomb stands conspicuous. The great men of this country, like the oaks of its forests, are of spontaneous growth. The hot-house of patronage, the adscititious aids of noble family and illustrious alliance, are not necessary to bring them to maturity. They invigorate and expand, as well amid the storms, as beneath the sunshine, of fortune...

The subject of this Memoir will be found, like most of his eminent countrymen, to have risen by the salient and recuperative energies of his own genius. Although born of respectable parents, and receiving, not an elaborate and finished, though highly valuable education, still he must be viewed as the architect of his own fortunes, the arbiter of his own destiny. How many, even in our own country, have enjoyed greater advantages, had more powerful connections, been educated at universities, and perfected in their studies by foreign travel, who yet have performed no deed of fame, and rendered no service to society. The prominence of station, the widespread and enduring celebrity, which Macomb has acquired, have been fairly earned in the open field of honorable competition and emulous prowess. He sowed the harvest which he reaps. By his own right arm, he plucked the laurels with which a nation garlands his brow, and which, in peace, like Harmodius, he weaves into a wreath where his sword reposes. Such a man

seems always favored by good fortune, because he wins it by
address, or commands it by boldness.

The subject of this memoir was born at Detroit, on the 3rd
of April 1782. Though not, like one of the heroes of antiquity,
born on a tapestry representing the scenes of the Iliad, he may
yet almost literally be said to have been nursed in field and for-
tress, and rocked by the storms of war. Detroit, at this time, was
a military post. The chubby boy became a favorite with the
soldiers of the garrison. He was dandled on the soldier's knee,
fed at the soldier's mess—his eye was dazzled with the gorgeous
pageantry of military parade—and his ear delighted with the
rousing strains of martial music. He slept and awoke amid
martial sounds and associations. External objects so readily
and deeply stamp their impression on the mind just opening, to
the world, it is not a matter of surprise that the dreams of his
infancy and the visions of his youth, were of military glory. . .

—Alexander Macomb, the Major General
Commanding the Army of the United States
by George H. Richards, Esq. Captain of Macomb's Artillery,
in the Late War (New-York: M'elrath, Bangs & Co., 1833).

• • •

John McCombs took off his spectacles and closed the book he
was reading about his cousin, now a famed and exalted war hero,
Alexander Macomb Jr. He could barely stomach the purple prose
and the adulation, let alone the contents therein. Yes, his cousin
Alexander's side had won, and the winners do write the history
books. He knew this much was true and couldn't very well argue
with it. But he couldn't for the life of him understand how someone from his own bloodline could fight for colonies. Though the

colonies had now been calling themselves the "United States of America" since the Revolution, like most loyal subjects, John could never stand behind such treason. His loyalty would forever be with the king of England. To distinguish and distance himself from his traitorous American cousin, John had changed his name from the standard styling of "Macomb" to "McCombs," as had his own father, Timothy, half brother to Alexander's father. Timothy had raised John and his siblings to be Loyalists—devoted to God and country alone.

"Brothers and kin be damned," his father, Timothy, had often said to John when he was a child. "They will bring you nothing but heartache and disappointment. Put your love in an exalted place, with God and with the king."

John had done just that. He believed his father and took his words as the gospel truth—a fact that made his father's ultimate betrayal all the more impossible to comprehend. Though, was it really so impossible to comprehend? John often wondered. His father all but told him "kin be damned." And in the end, damning his own children is indeed what he did.

For all of his talk of loyalty to the king, John's father, Timothy, was the real traitor to the Crown. He was an outlaw. A wanted spy. A "Patriot." Most of all, he was a disgrace to his son. Timothy was a coward in John's eyes. Instead of facing his fate—being drawn and quartered for his treasonous deeds—Timothy ran away, escaping across the border. When John had returned from the War of 1812, defeated and looking for solace from the one man whom he thought he could count on, he found his childhood home emptied, his father, mother, and all of his siblings gone. Worried that his family had been massacred, he ran to a neighbor's house, where he heard for the first time of his father's deplorable, unforgivable betrayal.

All the while when John had been fighting down the Patriots

and writing letters of his exploits to Timothy, telling him in rich
detail of the battles he had fought in, and more crucially, where
the British army units were headed next, Timothy had been hand-
ing those letters over to his half brother Alexander, the father of
Alexander Jr., the great and noble major general.

John's stomach turned when he first heard the awful news.

"You mean to say my own father turned over my letters to my
cousin, Major General Macomb?" he'd asked.

"It appears so," his neighbor Matthew Stuart said resolutely.
"His crimes were detailed in the decree of treason that was sent
throughout the provinces. There were eyewitnesses. The Royal
Army also had spies, one of whom witnessed your father turn over
a batch of your letters to his brother, who in turn passed them on
to his son, Major General Macomb."

"I don't understand," John said. "Why would my father put my
own—his own son's—life in peril? That of my men? Our country? How could a father—a man—do such a thing?"

"So much of what a man does or doesn't do is for the most part
a mystery to every other man. Your father is no different. Though,
if I were to wager a guess, I would say land had something to do
with it," Matthew said. "It's been known to turn brother against
brother, friend against friend, and even father against son. This
wouldn't be the first time."

"What do you mean?"

"I think your father stands to gain quite a sum of land in the
Americas," Matthew said. "I think his brother brokered some
kind of land deal."

"But what would my uncle Alexander get out of giving his
brother more land?" John asked.

"It's not what he 'gets'—it's what he 'got.' Your uncle was in a
fair lot of trouble in the Americas for a time and received many
favors from people in high places."

"So my uncle set up a spy ring in order to prove his own loyalty and pay back the country for his debts, and he somehow involved my father? He promised him land and no doubt something as silly as a title or a prominent position in the government?" John asked incredulously.

"It appears so."

"And my father would risk his own son for such a thing?"

"If it makes you feel any better, son, there was talk that in exchange for the letters and info, not only would the Macombs guarantee land in the Americas for you all, they would also make sure to spare you and set you up quite well, too," Matthew said quietly.

"Spare me? How on earth would they ensure that?" John asked.

"Orders were given to identify you and spare you on the American side . . ." The neighbor hesitated, as if holding back more information.

"And? What are you leaving out? What aren't you telling me?"

"Your commanding officer . . . he was a good friend of your father's," the neighbor said with a nod, trying to help John figure it out on his own.

John got up from his chair and paced the floor in the hopes of hastening the onset of understanding. There was a long pause. "You mean to tell me that my father was writing letters to the Royal Army and telling them to hold me back from battle?" John shook his head in agony. The very thought abhorred him.

His old neighbor shook his head too. "I think it is much worse than that."

John looked at the man quizzically. "What? What could be worse than my father intervening?"

The neighbor stayed silent as John worked through the possibilities on his own. Suddenly, John's eyes widened when the realization hit him. "No! No! I don't believe it! You think my father accused *me* of being the spy? You think he told the Royal Army that I was the one feeding him information—on purpose? No! No! Impossible!"

"I am so sorry, John. I am so sorry," the neighbor said, shaking his head again.

John turned to leave, unable to restrain his emotion any longer and unwilling to admit any further witnesses to his pain. Before he was halfway down the walkway, he stopped in his tracks and turned back.

"But they didn't believe him?" John asked, raising his voice to be heard over the distance now between himself and the other man.

"No," Matthew called back. "Your bravery on the battlefield apparently spared you from any suspicion, John. All those sacrifices you made for the Crown were well documented and witnessed. Your leadership in the burning of Buffalo, too. And everyone here knows about your care for General Brock—it's all well documented. We all read in the papers how you saw the brave general fall. Many witnesses observed you carrying his body to Fort George at Niagara. We know of your heroics at Niagara, Chippewa, Lundy's Lane, and Queenstown, too. You're a hero, John. A hero, and no one will ever think anything less than that of you. Not around here." As he'd spoken, the neighbor had made his way up to John and now stood before him, reaching out his hand to shake.

"Thank you," John said. "I'm sorry to have troubled you today."

"You're no trouble at all, John. In fact, why don't you come back inside, have some supper with us, and rest here until you figure out what you want to do."

"What do you mean, what I want to do?" John asked.

"Well, while you decide if you want to stay here or go find your father in America."

"I don't need to decide anything. My father made the decision for the both of us the minute he decided to use me in his dangerous game. I am staying here. Right here I'll live the rest of my days. To hell with him."

John was a man of his word. He never reached out to his father again. He took the two hundred acres that were awarded to him for his service and bravery in loyalty to the Crown, and he never looked back. That was until the present time, some twenty years later, when he learned of the publication of his cousin's biography and forced himself to read it. It would surprise John to learn that Alexander was able to admit that his success came in the most ignoble of ways. Of course, on some level, John knew the history books would never reveal such a thing. Major General Alexander Macomb's biographer most certainly would have left that detail out—namely the fact that he had more than a little help from his influential father vis-à-vis John's own father.

Though for the rest of his life after the war, John never attempted to reach out to his father, Timothy did try his best over the years to explain himself to his son in a series of letters. John kept only the first one he received, and he did so for one simple reason: It was indisputable proof, should there ever be any question of John's loyalty to the Crown.

My dear son, John,

I hope this letter finds you well and in good spirits. I am sure by now you know that we have our home and have settled in here in America, though I can't disclose our exact location yet. I am sure it is a shock to learn that your own father was indeed a Patriot and helped and supported the revolutionaries in their ultimate defeat of the British army. I hope someday you will see that, like all those called to fight in war, in the end the decision of which side to fight on was less about God and country, and more to do with family.

This, I know, may anger and hurt you more, for in the end, I chose to fight against my own son. I hope you understand how much more complicated the matter is. Hopefully this letter will help to serve as an explanation.

My entire life I sought the affection and approval of my older brothers and my own father. I did everything within my power to show them my admiration and love, and was met with nothing but contempt and disapprobation. It was only later, at my mother's deathbed, that I learned why my own brothers reviled me so. It had nothing to do with me. They hated me for the sins of my own father. I was a bastard, you see. Our father had an affair with a young woman not his wife or the mother of my brothers, who died in childbirth. Alas, the great mother who raised me was not my own. Yet she showered me with love and tenderness and treated me as if I were—much to the anger of my older siblings.

For most of my childhood, my brothers had no use for me. They went to Detroit and made their wealth in the fur trade. Alexander moved back East and made his fortune in land—before he lost it all in some bad business dealings. But, Alexander Hamilton came to his defense and brokered his release from debtors prison in exchange for a favor—in fact, repeated favors—favors that would help keep the newly formed United States government informed of the Crown's affairs. It seems my brother's fall from grace was not only a humbling experience for him, but one that put him in need of me, his long-forgotten brother, as well. If I could procure for him information about the movements and actions of the British forces, Alexander assured me I would be granted the land, freedom, and prestige that he himself enjoyed, and

quite possibly a position in the newly formed government. I thought it would be a wonderful new start for me, for my brothers, and for my own family as well. I was thinking only of your interests. I imagined being able to pass on land to you and your siblings. I imagined making a name for myself, as my brother had done.

Even after Hamilton was fatally shot in an absurd duel over political honor in 1804, my services were still required. I was their man on the edge. I had the information they so needed. I never meant to harm you or involve you. I never met to tell you until the time was right. But when you came of age and began to take my talk of being a Loyalist to heart, which as you now know was a cover so as to not be found out by our neighbors and friends, I was torn between my fidelity to my brother or to my son, not simply torn between two countries or allegiances.

So many times, you must believe me, I wanted to reach out and tell you. But I was so proud of you and your resolve of your convictions too. I knew you would survive, and I knew that after the war was eventually over, we would be reunited. It was my sincerest belief that after all the political quarrels between the two countries ended, we would be fine.

My truest hope is that you might one day forgive me. Please know I never meant to put you in harm's way. I realize now how naïve I was and what peril and danger I put you in. It wasn't until I myself was sentenced to being drawn and quartered that I realized the fate that could befall my own son as well. I am so sorry, son. If you ever find it in your heart to forgive me, I will be here and will spend the rest of my life making it up to you.

Forgive me,
Father

Forgiveness was not something John came to easily. He knew logically it was the right and Christian thing to do. But, there was a part of him that felt the love between him and his father was forever tainted. He had lost all respect for the man, and there was just no way he could go back now and forget it all happened.

He had witnessed too much, felt too much. He had watched his best friends die in battle. He saw them defeated—their bodies left bloodied and battered on what would someday become a forgotten battlefield. He felt anger and guilt. Had he not written those letters to his father, perhaps those men would have lived? Perhaps there would have been some way to save them. What more could have been done?

To read his cousin's cold words describing the dreadful day disgusted him: "I have the honor to inform you, that the British army, consisting of four brigades, a corps of artillery, a squadron of horse, and a strong light corps, amounting, in all, to about fourteen thousand men . . . are now retreating precipitately, leaving their sick and wounded behind." John thought of his friends, his brothers in arms, his true relations as they bled and moaned, being left behind.

The greatest victory for one is the greatest sorrow for another!

Before the war he was one of the king's chosen men kept to keep an eye on the colonies. Yes, he had fought valiantly—even against his own cousin at Plattsburgh. He always knew it was a possibility he would one day run into his cousin in battle. And he did, though his cousin would, of course, never recount such a thing in his illustrious biography.

No, Alexander would never admit defeat by a Canadian cousin born of his bastard uncle. Such things are best left unwritten, John knew.

John thought from time to time of writing his own memoir. There was so much life to tell. How did someone even begin to choose what memories or recollections should live on for posterity? And who would even care—after his children and grandchildren were gone, would anyone ever wonder who he, John McCombs, was or what he stood for? Did anyone care about those who lost the battles or the war? Did anyone remember those who simply lived lives of hard work and service, whose names would never be written down in the halls of history or in the annals of a military conflict?

Since the war had ended over twenty years ago, John had built a quiet but busy life for himself. He had traded in the two hundred acres of land, granted to him by the Crown after the war, for a tract of one hundred acres of even better land in Grantham. He had more than thirteen children—a legacy in and of itself.

No; he thought better of it—writing down his memories would be a waste. His memoir could not possibly contain all the glory and beauty of being a father to the many bright and ambitious minds he had been so gratified to be able to bring into this world. And besides, who would care anyway? Who would ever wonder what became of John McCombs?

7

LOVE HAS A WAY OF
SURPRISING YOU

*D*ouglas closed the book he was reading about his ancestor Timothy, the rebel spy who had deceived his own son, John. Douglas couldn't believe what he had just read.

"Isn't that something," he said out loud.

Suzy, who was nearby reading a book of her own, her feet tucked underneath her comfortably on her couch, looked up as she pulled her reading glasses down to the tip of her nose to look at Douglas. "Now what did you find out?" she asked.

Douglas had almost forgotten he was in Suzy's home. He thought he had been talking out loud to himself as he had many times in the past—forgetting all time and space as one so often does when reading. Besides, he had become so accustomed to living alone that recently he'd become routinely startled when he heard Suzy's voice next to him in the room.

"You all right, Douglas?" she asked, getting up and placing her book gently on the coffee table before walking across the room to stand next to him by the chair.

Douglas reached up, took her hand, and kissed it. He hadn't grown tired of this gesture. It had been several months now of dinners, movies, long walks, and Broadway shows. It was a slow courtship. A bit of a dance for both of them. As a divorcee, she was cautious to begin a new relationship, and as a private person she didn't reveal too much to begin with. He was cautious too, but *he did reveal* and liked to reveal everything. But somehow they worked. He liked to talk, and she liked to listen. He showed affection, and she willingly accepted it. Their first kiss had been a simple peck after their first date. He walked to the door, took her hands in his, and pulled her close as he bent down to kiss her. For their second, she took his hand as they walked to the restaurant, reaching up on her tippy toes to kiss him hello. On the occasion of the third, she invited him up for a cup of tea.

Eventually, they had reached the point in their relationship where they could do what most people do in long-term committed relationships: Simply sit in the same room and not have to talk. Just be together.

They did not have to fill the air with small talk or even explain themselves to each other. They could simply enjoy each other's company and presence without saying a word. They both liked to read. They both liked to go out to eat. They both liked to watch movies. It was simple. It was so easy. He didn't have to cajole her to go out. She didn't have to beg him to stay home. It was all new to Douglas, and he loved it.

Above all, Douglas liked being with Suzy in her apartment. It was warm and inviting there, and he felt relaxed. There were no memories of Hope there. In this new place, he could be a new version of himself. He could detach his mind from old stories and old expectations. He was finding out what he liked and what he didn't—on his own terms—and Suzy made that easy. Everything about being with her was easy. She laughed heartily at his jokes and observations. She didn't need fancy restaurants every night.

"Gosh, I am craving a hot dog. Let's go out on the street and find a vendor," she'd say to him as often as not.

She'd pull out the *Times* on Sunday and look over the shows. "Which one you interested in seeing? I'm up for anything."

Suzy absorbed experiences. She tasted every morsel of food. She listened to every note of a piece of music and danced to every beat—and boy, could she dance.

She surprised him every day with a fact she knew or a talent she had. She took ballroom dancing in the evenings and was quite good. She asked him to come and watch one of her competitions, and he sat in awe of her sheer physicality and the sleek lines her body made as she glided across the dance floor. She was so small and agile that her partner could spin her, pull her, push her, and lift her up as if she were attached to a buoyant string tethered to his hands. She seemed to snap back to him and roll away from him with ease. He wanted to dance with her, push her partner out of the way, pull her into his arms, and dance all night. But she was equally electrifying to watch. He could see the energy emanate around her. As a man of science, he knew all humans are made of energy and matter, but in his eyes she was *pure energy*—pure light. She glowed.

She was a woman of adventure and soul. She wanted to suck the marrow out of every bit of life. She read books from every genre. She wasn't ashamed or embarrassed to admit she liked drippy romances or predictable mysteries. Some of her pretentious and hifalutin colleagues would turn their noses up at the books she selected, but she didn't care. She knew what she liked, and she wasn't going to let someone's opinion dictate that.

She had learned early on that the opinions of others didn't make one very happy. All her life she had bent over backward to please her disapproving and tight-lipped mother, and over and over again she was met with indifference, if not downright insults.

A few months into their relationship, Douglas had met Suzy's mother and said to Suzy, "She's lovely. I don't know what you're talking about when you say she's difficult."

Suzy just rolled her eyes and shook her head as if to say, "Just you wait."

"What? She's so polite!" Douglas doubled down.

"That's because you're not her daughter—and you just paid for her dinner!" Suzy said and laughed.

Douglas didn't see it. He didn't understand the relationship. Like most men, he often found himself inadvertently dismissing a woman's perception of reality without any real basis for doing so. It wasn't until Suzy's dance competition, when she not only medaled but came in first place, that he understood and saw it with his own eyes.

Douglas was so proud and excited for her that he couldn't wait for Suzy to tell her mother. Surely this was something her mother could rejoice in and be happy about. Surely this was going to be something her mother would finally acknowledge.

Soon after the competition, both Suzy and Douglas took her mother out for Sunday brunch, and Douglas proudly reported the news.

"Hmph," Suzy's mother said as if it barely registered. "Can you pass the butter?"

Douglas looked at Suzy, who looked back at him with a smug expression as if to say, "I told you so."

Douglas was enraged. How could a person be so cold? So cutting? Didn't she see how wonderful Suzy was? How smart she was? How beautiful? How talented?

He couldn't wait for the brunch to end. He never wanted to look at or see *that woman* again. He wanted to wrap Suzy up in his arms and protect her for all time. He wanted to tell her that she was worthy and good and didn't need anyone's approval but her own. But something in Douglas told him she already knew that.

That's why Suzy danced. That's why Suzy read. Suzy had escaped the clutches of someone else's fanciful ideal for her a long time ago. She had taught herself how to be happy, how to feel loved, how to enjoy life—because she didn't have a mother to do that.

Later that day in the car, though, Douglas saw a side of Suzy that he never had before. She dropped her head and wept. Douglas was helpless and didn't know what to say or do to make her feel better.

"It's okay, Douglas. I'll be okay," Suzy reassured him. "This wasn't the first time. It's just who she is. Nothing I do will ever be good enough. Nothing I do will ever measure up." Suzy wiped the tears away from her cheeks and regained her composure.

"Well, she's certainly no prize," Douglas mumbled under his breath, making Suzy laugh again.

"Hey, she's still my mother. I can talk about her the way I want, but no one else can. I love her and that's that."

Right then, in that moment, Douglas knew how much he loved her. He loved her strength. He loved her courage. He loved her honesty. He loved her ability to forgive and accept her own mother, who was so unwilling to afford her the same courtesy or compassion. He didn't think he would ever be able to do such a thing himself. He could never love and accept anyone who would willingly harm the ones he loved. It hurt too much to watch Suzy suffer. He wanted to do everything he could to make her happy, to make her see just how amazing and beautiful she was—no matter what anyone else thought or said.

• • •

He wanted to spend every minute he could with Suzy, but she worked Monday through Friday. Nevertheless, Douglas made the most of every minute he could find to be with her. Over the past several months they had developed a bit of a routine. He'd walk to the library and eat lunch with her, and then he would sit in the park and read for a bit or run errands, and when it was quitting time, he returned and walked her home. Sometimes he cooked dinner. Sometimes, she did. Sometimes they went out.

After three months or so of this, they still had not yet spent the night at each other's places. Douglas didn't even know how to ask for such a thing. Sure, he wanted to be with her. He wanted to spend every night, every minute of the day with her, but he also didn't want to ruin it or be too forward. Sex wasn't something that he felt he could bring up.

But when he was asked to speak at an event in Los Angeles, he invited Suzy to come along so she could check out a few dance events and take in some sights.

"I'd get two rooms, of course," Douglas said.

"One will be just fine," Suzy said. The look on her face spoke volumes.

She was ready. He was ready.

Now, all these months later, they were every bit a couple. He hadn't thought it was possible to be this happy again. He hadn't thought it was possible to love like this again—or, if he were being honest—for the first time. The love he'd had with Hope was different. This was new. But love has a way of surprising you in the infinite ways it manifests itself. The heart was always surprising him. Just when he thought couldn't love any more, the heart found a way. Love is tenacious like that.

The first time he told her "I love you," Douglas felt it in his heart. His chest expanded, and he felt his windpipe clench. His entire body seized with emotion and he couldn't contain it all. It wanted to burst through him and explode into an infinite number of stars.

After they were long gone, who would remember this love? Douglas wondered. *Where would all that energy and light go? Did it expand out into the infinite to dance among the stars?*

But these moments of absolute euphoria were brief. When he was with her he was so grounded and firmly placed in the present, all he could feel was love and joy, but when he was away from her at his own home, he would be jolted, as if awakened from a blissful night's sleep into a waking nightmare.

Every time he left Suzy and found himself alone, he would be flooded with old feelings and old thoughts. It was as if his mind were intent on betraying him, over and over again. *Why bother loving her if it's all going to end anyway?* he thought. And then immediately he'd even feel guilty for falling in love again at all. *Aren't I betraying Hope by moving on?* He had always said that he would rather die, rather give his own life for Hope, but here he was alive. *Did that mean I never really loved her at all?* Or did the meaning he had always ascribed to love change now too? Could love do that? Change? And did the measure of love have to be giving one's life? Was there more to it than that?

Of course, on a rational level, he knew that it was impossible for anyone to take Hope's place. She had Alzheimer's. He could've stepped in front of a bullet for her, but he couldn't transfer minds. There was no way to go back in time and take her place. And no, he knew, there was no betrayal in moving on, either. Hope, the Hope he had known and fallen in love with decades ago, was no longer there. But he couldn't help but feel society's cold gaze and harsh judgments. So many movies and so many books all glorify and romanticize the intertwining lives of couples deeply in love who ultimately die in each other's arms, or the partner that succumbs to a broken heart so shortly after the passing of their beloved. But what about those left behind, as he had been? Were they allowed to move on? Did they *dare?*

How dare anyone move on after love. How dare anyone get up and pick up the pieces of their shattered heart? How dare anyone continue walking over the glistening shards that remain, that cut and make you bleed as you continue to move forward?

• • •

But on this day in Suzy's living room reading a book about Timothy and his son John, everything was going so well. Later they would walk to dinner, and later still, he would lie next to her in bed and hold her as she drifted off to sleep. He didn't want anything to disrupt this. He didn't want those old thoughts to come in.

But, there were things he was keeping from Suzy. He had more in common with his ancestor Timothy than he could ever have imagined. Timothy spent his whole life telling his son what love and loyalty was. He told his son it was laying down one's life for the Crown. But in the end, Timothy didn't do that. He started a new life, in a new place, and he faced judgment and ridicule for it. His own son could never forgive him for such a betrayal. All the infinite love in the world couldn't bring the father and son back together. What was that like for Timothy to stand in a new truth, a new land? And what was it like for John to feel so betrayed by his own father? Douglas felt for John too. John had wondered about what sort of legacy he would leave for his children and grandchildren's children—for people like Douglas.

"What was so interesting?" Suzy was asking Douglas again.

Douglas stuttered, finding it impossible to answer. He wanted to tell her the story of his great ancestor's betrayal, but he was afraid of where the story would lead. Every time he brought up the past, they both started talking about their own, and she would invariably point out all the ways he was so much like his ancestors. He didn't want to be like these ancestors. Not now.

He didn't want to bring up family secrets. He didn't want to bring up betraying the people he loved the most. He wanted to protect her, to keep her safe, to make sure that no one judged or disapproved of her the way others had—especially her own mother. He wanted to spare her the fate of his own legacy.

More than anything, he wanted to spare her the grief and pain not only of inevitable loss, but of damning judgment, too. He loved her so much now, the thought of losing her overwhelmed him.

And there was something, something she should know, something he had to tell her, but if he did, he could lose it all, and he wasn't ready to do that. No, he absolutely couldn't do that.

He hadn't come this far, he hadn't learned this much, and he hadn't fallen in love again to let it all disappear and blow up in an instant.

"Nothing, just some more Macomb/McCombs military history. Nothing you'd be too interested in. Ready to go find something for dinner?" Douglas said rather quickly.

"Sure," Suzy said with a smile.

Douglas looked at her and knew that though she said, "Sure," something deep inside her knew that Douglas was keeping something from her. Yes, women always know when they're not getting the whole story. But Douglas knew her too well by now. She would never push him, never force him to feel anything or say anything. She didn't want to lose him either. Things were good. Things were solid. She had said it over and over again to him, "For the first time in my life, I feel completely loved and taken care of." He didn't want to change that. And if it meant keeping her in the dark about something, it's what had to be done.

"Everyone has secrets," Suzy once said. "Everyone." Douglas had always taken that to mean that she had a few of her own, too.

"Well, let's get a move on it," Douglas said, snapping his book shut resolutely and throwing it down on the coffee table.

"Careful! That's a library book!" Suzy said sharply.

"My apologies, Ms. Librarian." Douglas bowed.

They both laughed and headed toward the door.

The secrets could wait for a little while.

8

REV. JACOB McCOMBS

Great-grandfather of Douglas McCombs

———

Born May 14, 1825, in Dunnville, Ontario, Canada

Died December 30, 1911, Dunnville, Ontario, Canada

Son of John and Magdalene Macomb of Ontario

Grandson of Timothy and Sarah McCombs

Great-grandson of John Macomb and an Unknown Mother

*F*rom a young age, Jacob knew he wasn't like his siblings. It was quite a feat, in fact, as there were thirteen children in all, and it was true that not one was quite like him. Most of them were industrious and capable. His father, John, had a large farm and needed as many hands as possible to run it. Jacob was just one of the many hands that made for light work, though he knew he wasn't much of a help. As one of the middle children, Jacob was preceded by stronger brothers and more socially advanced and cunning sisters.

In contrast to his siblings who took after their stalwart father, Jacob resembled his small-framed mother. He was small in stature, thin, bookish, and quiet like her as well. He would have much preferred to stay inside during the harsh Ontario winters and read. He showed little interest in courting girls when the time came, and only did so at the urging of his mother and sisters, who thought it was unnatural that he preferred to stay indoors and read incessantly. Though his mother and sister preferred novels, he preferred to read philosophy, and he was particularly fond of the Bible. In fact, from a young age, he felt called to serve God and others. There was never a question of what he wanted to be when he grew up, he always just *knew*. He was a servant of God, though he found it difficult to find the courage to tell his parents that he had no interest in ever becoming a farmer.

Instead, he quietly began to teach himself. Whenever he picked up the Bible and removed himself from his family's raucous banter and card playing after meals, his older brothers and sisters would just roll their eyes at him. They didn't dare tease him, lest they face the wrath of their father, who for all of his talk of wanting his own children to become farmers like him, didn't mind when his son Jacob showed an early proclivity for life as a minister.

"The world could use some people with a little common decency," John would often scold the other children when they rolled their eyes.

Yes, he loved his son Jacob. In truth, he loved all of his children.

John was trying desperately to not repeat the sins of his own father. Before his children were all born, he made a personal vow that he would never lie to them. He would never pretend to be something other than who he was. He would never betray them or make them feel abandoned or disgraced. He felt a father had only one job, and that job was to support and unconditionally love *all* his children. Just because Jacob was different, a little odd he had to admit, if only privately, he would never withhold his abundant love for his son. He would never stop defending him. John believed that the heart's ability to love was infinite—a parent could love his first child as much as his thirteenth. No child was more important or more special than all the rest.

Jacob felt that love—the love between a father and his son— the same kind of love he read about in the Bible. And just as his savior Jesus Christ was devoted to God the Father, Jacob worshipped his own. He admired his stoicism, his grace, his wisdom, and his strength. He admired his ability to love all of his children well and equally. Jacob aspired to be just like him—to be able to give without ever expecting anything in return.

When Jacob finally had the courage to tell his father he wanted to go to divinity school, he asked his father to take a walk with him. They got up early and headed out from the McCombs homestead before dawn. The night before, Jacob had said he needed to discuss something privately, and with so many people underfoot he didn't want their conversation to be disturbed.

John didn't have to be told twice. He knew what his son was going to ask, but he went along with it anyway because he knew it was important to Jacob.

He let Jacob fumble a bit—and listened as the young man tried to make small talk. When they were far enough away from home, John turned to Jacob. "Out with it, son."

"I don't want to be a farmer, Father. I—I have been called by God."

John put his hand on his son's shoulder and gave him his blessing.

"I've only had one wish for my children," John said to his son.

"What's that?" Jacob asked.

"That you use the skills the good Lord gave you," John replied.

Jacob smiled and nodded.

"You have something in you, Jacob, that wants to know more and desires to be of service. Those aren't accidents. God gave you those as gifts to use and to help other people. Who am I to stand in the way of what the Lord has intended for you?"

Jacob nodded and smiled again, feeling so much gratitude and love for the man who raised him.

"We will miss you. But it's best if you go away and study. You can always come back, anytime you wish. You'll always be welcome here. And we're never going anywhere. So, what will you be needing from me?"

Jacob held out the letter from the divinity school in Cambridge.

"In *England*?"

"Yes, Father. I thought it would be best to study there. I will just need money for passage. My studies are paid for in exchange for service to the Church of England."

"I can arrange for that, son," John said without expression.

"Are you angry, Father?" Jacob asked.

"Angry? *Angry?* Why would you think that?"

"Because I am going so far away," Jacob said.

"I think it's wonderful. I was just thinking how fitting it is that one of my sons would go back to where we came from. What a miracle it all is, really."

"Didn't our ancestors come from Scotland?" Jacob asked, confused.

"Yes, a long time ago. But our service has been to the Crown. I fought for England a long time ago, and it's fitting that at least one of my children should be able to see what it was we were fighting for. You will be able to fulfill a dream I had for myself but will most likely never see come true. I suppose one of the greatest legacies a person can leave behind for their children are their own unfulfilled dreams," John mused.

"Why's that?" Jacob asked.

"So that my children can live a life I only dreamed of. Every generation gets a new chance. There are dreamers and there are doers in this life, Jacob. I don't know—maybe it skips a generation! But you're no dreamer. You're a doer. You don't just read the books, you apply them. You don't just talk about becoming a minister, you're going to do it!"

"Look what you have created. You're a decorated war hero, a large property owner, a father to thirteen, and a devoted husband. And you were the mastermind behind the great Welland Canal! Because of you, this entire area prospered," Jacob said.

"Yes, yes, yes." John laughed. "I think that's a bit of stretch. I just gave some ideas about how they might go about digging. Anyone could do such a thing," John said, diminishing his own contributions.

"That's not true, Father! You have been called a genius! You do not even have an engineering degree, but you came up with a way to bypass Niagara Falls! No other man could have conceived of such a thing."

John shook his head. "It was nothing."

"*Nothing?* Why do you always do that?" Jacob asked. "Why can't you accept praise or glory? Aren't you the one who said that God gives us skills and it is our duty to use them? Do you not diminish God when you refuse to accept that you used your God-given talents to help others?"

John smiled and shook his head and then wagged his finger at Jacob. "Ah, children are so good at turning things around and using a parent's advice against them."

Jacob smiled and said, "You have just done so much. I want you to know that I have seen it—and that your children have seen it, and someday, generations from now will remember you—not just as a dreamer, but a doer."

John nodded. "Thank you for that, son. But I had dreams too. Dreams that I know I will not see in my lifetime. Dreams that I had to pass on to my own children, so they could live them."

"Like going to England?"

"Yes."

"You could still go. You could come and visit me!" Jacob said excitedly.

"And leave the farm? Your brothers and sisters? No. Don't be silly. A man has responsibilities. Dreams are to be pursued—only if they don't cause someone else to lose theirs. I would never put my own dreams before those of my children. Do you understand?"

"Yes, Father."

"So go now while you're young. Explore the world as much as you can. Take it all in. There is so much to see beyond the confines of our little farm. We come from a long line of dreamers—of explorers with intrepid minds. I don't know it *for a fact*, but I feel it. The books I have read about the men who fought on the fields of Culloden told me these were brave men—loyal men. They believed in a calling higher than themselves. Then there were our ancestors who came to a New World despite knowing nothing of what they would find here. They were buoyed by a dream of a better life for their family and their ancestors. Even my own father . . ." John trailed off.

Jacob's eyes widened. He and all of his siblings were forbidden to ever speak of their grandfather Timothy. It was their mother who told them the story of their grandfather's betrayal, how he was a spy and chose another country over his own sons. The children were warned never, ever to ask about him or talk about him.

"Go on, Father, finish. What were you going to say about your father?"

John took a deep breath. "As much as it pains me to say this, because it causes me so much regret and guilt, I loved my father. Yes, his betrayal hurt me. But as I have grown older and have children of my own, I have come to understand him a little better. I have come to see his dreams—how big they were, how expansive. He just wanted so much for us. He also thought he knew what was best. I can look back on it all now and see he was just doing the best he could."

"Are you saying you are ready to forgive him?" Jacob asked quietly, speaking already as a minister would.

"Forgiveness is a tall order, son. I don't pretend to be saintly. I still have so much anger. But yes, I suppose if understanding why someone does something is part of forgiveness, then I am getting there. Though he is no longer here for me to tell him such a thing. So there really is no point." John blinked back the tears gathering in his eyes.

"Forgiveness doesn't require the participation of the person in need of forgiveness," Jacob said. "It requires only *your* heart. When you forgive others, you free yourself from the suffering— that you alone have felt, anyway."

John nodded. "You're a wise man, Jacob."

Jacob shrugged it off, incapable of accepting a compliment, a trait his own father passed on to him—along with all of his dreams.

"Father, are you sure you won't be needing me?"

"Of course not. We have plenty of help here. But, would you promise me something?"

"Yes, Father, anything."

"Promise me you will forgive me someday."

"Forgive *you*? For what? What have you ever done that would require forgiveness from me or any of your children?"

"There are so many ways a parent can disappoint his children. In fact, I am sure there are an infinite number of ways. And one thing has always haunted me a bit—something from the Bible, actually."

"What's that?"

"The Bible asks God to 'forgive us our trespasses as we forgive those who have trespassed against us.' I have held grudges, son. I let my father die without ever sending him a kind word. I wonder now; will God return the favor? Will he not forgive me because I have not forgiven? The Bible also says, 'Do unto others as you would have done unto you.' Am I to suffer the same fate as my own father? Will one of my children turn their back on me? Refuse to forgive me for some harm done because I have done so to my own father? Are we all bound by the sins of those who have gone before us?" John asked contemplatively.

"Father, I would forgive you for anything. A thousand times I would forgive you. You never have to fear that. I will always be there for you."

"Yes, *you* will forgive me," John agreed. "You have a good heart and a good head. But what about your brothers and sisters?"

"Do you have a quarrel with any of them that I don't know?" Jacob asked.

"Not yet. But I fear the time is coming."

"I don't understand, Father. What are you talking about? Why would my brothers and sisters turn against you? There's nothing you could ever do to make them love you any less."

"We'll see about that," John said, looking off into the distance over the farm, the fields shimmering with morning dew in the gathering light of dawn.

"I have to leave this farm to one child," John said, choking a bit on the words. A lump formed in his throat and he tried to swallow.

"We all know that, Father. But that is so far off. You mustn't trouble yourself with such worries. Besides, we all know that you will leave it to the oldest, Timothy. We all understand that. There are no quarrels among us."

John turned his back from Jacob. He crossed his arms and began to walk away.

"He's the oldest son, Father! Right? Of course you'll leave it to Timothy. We all know that," Jacob said, repeating himself, trailing after his father.

John shook his head and pursed his lips.

"What? Father? What? What aren't you telling me?"

"I thought I could love him. I thought that by naming him after my own father, I could get closer to forgiving his betrayals. I thought I would be able to restore integrity to the name Timothy McCombs."

"What are you saying, Father? You don't love Timothy? You're not leaving the farm to him? I am confused."

"Your brother is in trouble, Jacob. Serious trouble. I don't know how to help him or even if I can help him."

"With the law?"

"No. He has gotten a girl—a young girl—with child."

"Oh, I see." Jacob nodded before John could finish saying the words.

"There has never, ever been any talking of common sense to the boy. He does as he pleases. I blame his mother. She doted on him so as a boy. She let him get away with everything. And now it seems there is no getting him out of this trouble he is in."

"Can't he marry the girl? Go to the next county and marry her? Surely he wouldn't be the first man in town to do so?"

"He can't marry her," John spat quickly, his temperament finally showing itself.

"Well, why not? Where is she? He hasn't been courting anyone since he got back from his work on the canal, not that I've seen anyway." Then Jacob realized something. "Oh no! He got a girl in trouble while he was working on the canal this summer?"

"Yes, of all the girls in the world, your brother Timothy has fallen for an Irish towman's daughter."

"She's a *Catholic*, then?" Jacob asked.

John nodded solemnly, as Catholicism was among the most egregious of offenses. He might as well have said, "She's a murderer, then." In both their minds, and in the minds of most loyal English subjects, a Catholic was immeasurably more offensive.

"Oh," Jacob said solemnly, suddenly understanding the gravity of his father's problem.

"Timothy loves her. He came home to ask for our blessing to marry her," John said somewhat incredulously.

"What are you going to do?"

"I can't do it," John said, shaking his head. "I can't do it, knowing I will be damning his soul to hell and knowing that his life will be ruined. All my hopes and dreams for him will be dashed. And his poor mother? What's to become of her? She's beside herself. The thought of her losing her son to an Irish Catholic girl. The thought of him turning his back on this farm, to run off with a girl he barely knows. To turn his back on all we have done for him and all we have given him!" John buried his head in his hands.

"Father, Father!" Jacob implored. "No! He *hasn't* turned his back. He loves a girl, that's all. Yes, he has sinned, but sins can be forgiven! You know that now! You said it yourself."

"No! No! Jacob, I can't forgive this. I can't. All of this," John said, throwing back his arms, "I did all of this for him. I wanted to leave him—my oldest, my progeny—this farm for generations, *his* generations."

"Father, please. There is no reason why you can't do that now. Let him marry the girl, bring her here. We can love the child."

"She refuses to leave her family. She insists on raising the child as a Catholic."

"No!" Jacob said, putting his hands over his mouth to hide the shock.

"Yes."

"So Timothy is leaving? You are disinheriting him?"

"Yes."

"And since I am leaving . . . and will become part of the Church of England . . . I will not be able to receive the land . . ." Jacob recited aloud dully, now fully realizing his father's pain. "So it will go to *James*?"

"Yes." John nodded dejectedly.

Jacob shook his head. James was brawny and large, a good farmhand, but he didn't have the mental capacity to run the farm or keep it profitable. "You're worried, aren't you, Father? You don't think James is up to the task? And you fear that if you give him the land, you will break Timothy's heart. He will never forgive you. Is that it?"

John looked at his son quietly and nodded.

"I understand. I am sorry, I had no idea. If I knew any of this, I wouldn't have come to you today with this." Jacob shook the letter in his hand.

"No. Don't you apologize. You've done nothing wrong. You make me proud, and you have never caused me any worry. I am grateful for that. This is your dream. This is your calling. I cannot and will not stand in the way."

"And what if Timothy's calling is to be the husband of an Irish Catholic? What if it is to be a father to this child?"

John shook his head. "There you go again flipping things. Using my own advice against me," John said with a smile.

"We will find a way to work things out," Jacob said, resolved.

John shrugged and looked exhausted. It was so tiring to worry this much.

"We don't need to figure out everything today. I know you love Timothy. And he knows you do too. Let him go to the girl. Every child needs a father. Timothy will be a good one. He learned from the best," Jacob said, wrapping his arm around his father's shoulders. Together, they headed back toward the McCombs homestead.

9

EVERYONE HAS SECRETS

*D*ouglas pulled the covers off of him gently, trying not to disturb Suzy as he got up out of bed. She was breathing deeply by now, but he couldn't join her in sleep. Something had been gnawing at him since dinner. Douglas could tell that Suzy was holding something back. *It takes one to know one.* The telltale signs were there. She wasn't forthcoming when he asked her direct questions about her ex-husband. She answered in generalities. "It was a difficult time." Or she quickly changed the subject. "Are you hungry? I'm starving. Let's order."

However, he couldn't help but wonder about what she'd said a few weeks prior. They had been talking about family secrets, and she had said, "Everyone has secrets." Naturally he had his own, but before that moment he hadn't thought that Suzy had hers. But the way she'd said it helped him realize that perhaps she had a few secrets of her own. Was she inviting Douglas to ask about them? Was she trying to tell him something? She was always so direct and honest, but tonight she hadn't been. The way she'd averted her eyes, he could tell she was holding onto something. What was she holding back from him? He wanted to press her, but he was afraid of the answer. But at the same time, the idea of being kept in the dark about her past terrified him. He didn't want anything to mar this relationship, the way secrets had tainted his life with Hope.

Hope had kept secrets from him. That was her way. She knew very well she didn't want to have children with him, but she also knew how much it meant to him that he someday become a father. So she kept it a secret to herself until after their wedding night. She went to great extremes to procure measures to prevent pregnancy. A condom wasn't enough—she used spermicides, cervical caps, and when the pill became available, she used that, too. She never revealed to him why, and she refused to answer his pleas for a reason, letting him blame himself instead.

"Is it because you don't love me? Is that why you don't want a child with me?" he asked once.

She let the question go without an answer, allowing the silence serve as a stout reply. But the real reason he would never know.

She kept that a secret, too.

Fearful Hope would leave him if he pressed her too hard for an answer, he acquiesced. He didn't push her to answer. He didn't require any explanations from her for anything. He loved her. He wanted to be with her. If it meant giving up his own dream to be a father, then so be it. Love, he knew, sometimes requires that you give up on your own dreams so another can have theirs. Somewhere he had heard that—or witnessed it. Sacrifice is all he knew of love. If you loved someone—you gave it all for them—your dreams, your life. And so he did. He gave up his one true dream to be a father so that Hope could live hers.

As the years went on, he realized her decision not to have a child had consequences. People judged her. Though it caused him pain not to have children, and he couldn't understand her reasons, he couldn't abide anyone else judging her. He would tell others: "It was all my fault." Soon he came to believe it. Douglas would often think, *If I had been a better husband, she would have wanted to have a child with me. If I was there. If I hadn't left for that meeting. If I hadn't traveled. If I just loved her a bit more. If I only . . .*

The self-flagellation gave him an odd sense of comfort and relief. If he blamed himself, he could somehow master the moment. He could regain some semblance of control of the situation. If *he* was at fault, *he* could do things that could change the situation. He could buy her another house—one in Switzerland, then one in Vienna, then one in Tuscany. He could throw yet another elaborate party on her behalf. He could put her at center stage, the way she liked it. He could shower her with gifts and flowers. He could have statues erected in her honor.

Yes, when he blamed himself, he could be in control again, but when he was actually *with* Hope, he was utterly unmoored. For all of his attempts to please, she could never be satisfied, and she was not easily wooed. This, too, was a secret he kept from everyone. The shame of it was too great to bear. Their friends and family saw smiling Hope, gracious Hope, the belle of every ball he threw. But at home, he experienced another Hope—a discontented and jealous Hope. She was needy and dependent. He waited on her. He doted on her, and yet she was *still* unhappy. Nothing he ever did was enough. *He was never enough.* From the outside, they had a romance of the century. They lived a life most would be envious of, but inside the four walls of their home, if he was being absolutely honest with himself, he felt trapped in so many ways. He was like the child crying out in the night for his parents to come for him, to love him, to pick him up and carry him to safety—but no one was coming to save him. No, Douglas never had anyone come to save him, no one to return the love and affection he so freely and selflessly gave. *Love me,* his heart cried out. *Just love me. Why can't you love me?*

Though Douglas had known Suzy for over six months now and though she had proven time and time again that she was a woman so very different from Hope, Douglas couldn't break his old habits. Hope had taught him to be distrustful. Hope had taught him to believe that all women kept secrets. Hope had taught him that he was responsible for another's happiness—and therefore unhappiness. He couldn't simply change who he was overnight. He had become just as dependent on Hope in some ways. He needed her to feel important. He needed her to feel like his life had meaning. He needed her so he could have someone to please. As much as he wanted to admit this wasn't true, it was. It's what he had always known his entire life, and changing that way of thinking wasn't easy—no matter how healthy, strong, and balanced this new relationship with Suzy was now.

Starting over with someone new, someone so completely different, was challenging. There was simply so much that Suzy didn't know about Douglas, and vice versa. For all of his marriage's weaknesses, at least Douglas knew what to expect day in and day out. There was comfort in the familiarity. Their roles were defined. But now Douglas was having to create a new life for himself, and in the meantime, a new way of thinking as well. Suzy was opening his eyes to all sorts of possibilities in life—possibilities that he didn't even know existed before he met her. Before, love was a chase. Hope was always just outside his grasp. But now, with Suzy, love was something you could hold onto. It was something both parties felt mutually. He was learning to be on the receiving end of joy. He felt like someone was there—for him. Yes, for the first time in his life, he felt safe.

This was equally wonderful and terrifying, because now he had so much to lose. A year ago this life had seemed unfathomable. He hadn't wanted to wake up each morning. He was waiting for God to take him. On the coldest night of the year, he walked out of his house without a coat on and kept walking. Without thinking, he found himself at the bench in Central Park where he had sat with Hope and held her hand during one of their happier times. It was freezing out. He just wanted it all to end. He wanted to sit on that bench and let the cold grip him from the outside to match the

cold, vast emptiness he felt on the inside. He wanted the pain and
the longing for Hope—for love, for anything at all—to just end. If
he was nothing with her, he was less than nothing without her. He
prayed the end would come quickly.

When Mark showed up, Douglas was nearly unconscious. He
was in the late stages of hypothermia. His body was no longer shiv-
ering. Unbeknownst to him, his internal organs were beginning to
slow and shut down. His heart, which had been beating rapidly
to keep warm just a few minutes before, had now slowed to a
dangerous, nearly imperceptible rhythm. His blood pressure was
beginning to drop. His muscles felt rigid. He could barely move.
He had a desperate urge to close his eyes and fall asleep. *I just want
to sleep. Not wake up.* He no longer felt the cold. His body and his
mind were at the brink of shutting down permanently.

"Douglas! Douglas! I've been looking all over for you! One of
your neighbors said they saw you head out for a walk without a
coat. What are you doing? We have to get you inside."

"Leave me be, Mark. Leave me alone. There's nothing left,"
Douglas whispered, his voice so dry it cracked as he spoke.

"Stop it, Douglas. Stop this. Let's get you inside. Here, take
my coat." Mark took his long black overcoat off and wrapped it
around Douglas's broad shoulders. The coat barely covered the
width of his back.

"Mark, why?"

"Why *what*? Come on, stand up." Mark looped his head underneath Douglas's arm and attempted to lift him up.

"Why am I here? How did I get here?" Douglas asked.

"You walked," Mark said resolutely.

"No, I mean, *why am I here on earth*? Why am I *alive*? What's
the point of it all?" Douglas mumbled weakly.

"You're here to live. You're here to love," Mark said resolutely.

"Well, I did that. I'm done, thank you very much."

"Let's get you home and get something warm inside you. Have you eaten today?"

"No," Douglas said, lifting himself and moving on his own. He didn't want to hurt Mark or be a burden to him, either.

"Okay, let's get you home and get a hot meal in you. You'll feel better."

"A hot meal isn't going to fix me, Mark. Why do people always think feeding grieving people is the answer?" Douglas asked. "They bring casseroles and food. They tell people: Eat. Just eat! As if food is the answer to all of life's problems."

"It's the answer to some of them," Mark said with a smile. "But I know what you mean. Sometimes it's the only way people can show they care. *Food is care.* I think it's hard for people to show they love each other, but food shows it without the words."

Douglas stopped and looked at Mark quizzically. "You care? You care about *me?*"

"Of course I care about you, Douglas! I care about you a great deal. You're one of my closest and best friends. I'd be lost with you."

"Really?" Douglas shook his head. "I don't think I matter very much at all."

"That's where you're wrong, Douglas. I know you think that Hope was all you had in life. But she made you think you were nothing, that you didn't matter. I don't think that. A lot of people don't think that. All the people whose lives you saved with your inventions, they think you matter too, a great deal in fact."

Douglas let Mark take care of him that night. He let Mark order him food. He let Mark sit and watch him eat. He let Mark care for him. He could tell it was important to Mark, and he didn't want to disappoint his friend. He didn't want to be any trouble for anyone. That's the last thing he ever wanted. His whole life he'd wanted to be the opposite of that. He wanted to be of service. And so, even in his darkest moment, he let Mark think he was helping.

And now all these months later, he was with a beautiful woman who cared about him. *Really* cared about him. She showed him love and affection. She showed him patience and care. And he might lose it all again should he pry too deeply into her secrets or should he reveal his own.

This is how secrets remain secrets, Douglas realized. No one ever thinks they're going to keep them forever. No one ever sets out hoping to deceive another or hurt another. But fear of losing someone, fear of losing love, fear of being alone is so primal, so innate, it overpowers all else. Every family has them. Every person has at least one—one part of themselves that will never be revealed to another human being. And perhaps it is best this way, he pondered. There are things he never wanted to know that Hope kept from him and that he ultimately discovered—only to break his heart and crush him. Perhaps it was best to keep things to oneself. Perhaps some secrets are too painful, too raw for another to have to partake in the burden of hearing.

Perhaps Suzy loved him so much she didn't want him to know the secrets of her past. That's why he didn't want to tell her his secret. He didn't want to hurt her. He didn't want to cause her any more pain and suffering.

Douglas was now pacing the floor. He played her words over and over: "Everyone has secrets." *What was* her *secret? What was it that she wasn't telling him? What was she trying to protect him from?*

"Douglas, what's wrong? Come back to bed," Suzy said, rolling over and lifting up the bedding to invite him back in.

"I can't sleep. I am sorry to bother you. You go back to bed," he said, walking to her side of the bed and bending over to kiss her.

"You look worried, Douglas," she said quietly. "Is there anything I can do? Anything I can get you? Do you want me to make you a snack? Do you need something to eat?"

Douglas smiled. She was trying to show she cared. And oh how she cared for him.

"I'm fine. You go back to sleep now. I'll just go out into the living room and read for a bit," he said, kissing her again.

"All right. But not too late," Suzy said, flipping over and snuggling deeper into her covers.

Suzy fell back to sleep quickly, unbothered. Perhaps her secrets were just a product of his own imagination. Perhaps *I am projecting? I'm the one with the secret, after all. Was it fair to assume she was keeping one?*

Perhaps she had nothing more to say about her ex. She had said all there was to say. She was over it. She was that type of person. He had seen it firsthand. She'd rather have peace than drama. She'd rather move on, eyes straight ahead, than look back on a dark and painful past. She was left with nothing after her marriage—no alimony, no education. She'd had to build a life all on her own. She forgave the man. She had said that, and she had moved on. Douglas had no reason not to believe it. He witnessed her forgiving and kind heart day in and day out. She was so happy and friendly to even the most undeserving of library visitors. She had the patience of a saint with her mother. She asked for so little of others. He knew these were all facts. But still, there was something inside her she was holding onto. Some pain he could almost feel. They had become so connected and so entwined, it was almost as though they no longer needed words to communicate. He just *knew* she was holding something back.

But what if she told him something he didn't want to hear? What if she had done something he didn't want to know? What if it could ruin everything?

Secrets had destroyed his ancestors. It had destroyed his own family, his own heart. Could he go through that again? Is knowing the past—the truth—more important than feeling peace and living in the present?

10

Norman Archibald McCombs

Grandfather of Douglas McCombs

———

Born July 17, 1851, in St. Catharines, Lincoln Co., Ontario, Canada
Died May 12, 1938, Haldimand Co., Ontario
Son of Rev. Jacob McCombs and Mary Ann (Bessey) McCombs
Grandson of John and Magdalene Macomb of Ontario
Great-grandson of Timothy and Sarah McCombs

*N*orman "Normie" McCombs was a lonely child. His father, Rev. Jacob McCombs, was an itinerant minister who served his congregation throughout St. Catharines and Lincoln County. His poor mother died in childbirth bearing him, and he had no siblings. The majority of his childhood was spent sitting on a church pew looking up at his father as he read from Scripture and gave long sermons about the importance of loving-kindness, forgiveness, and peace. His father was a quiet and studious man who preferred to read by the fire in the evening and go on long, quiet walks in the woods during the day. Neither option appealed much to young Normie. He didn't care to be alone; he wanted to be with other people. He wanted to play with other children. More than anything in the world, he longed for a mother to hold him and look after him. So young Normie lived for the summertime, because that was when his father took him back to his childhood home—a large farm filled with aunts and uncles, raucous cousins, and endless hours of fun.

Normie's father, Jacob, was a kind and smart man, but he was in no way affectionate. Normie never recalled receiving a hug from his father or a kiss goodnight. Normie only knew of these sorts of affectionate gestures because when he was at his grandfather's homestead in the summer, he watched as his cousins were embraced by their mothers, kissed on the forehead by their fathers on their way to bed, and curled up in their parents' laps when they were tired and in need of attention. All of these sights astonished the young boy. The closest Normie came to any form of affection from his father was when they kneeled beside each other at bedtime. Normie could feel his father's arm, raised in prayer, lean against his own arm as they both rested their elbows on the side of Normie's bed. It was only the slightest touch and the briefest of encounter, but Normie treasured it all the same.

Jacob wasn't cold or harsh; he simply didn't have a parental instinct. He had been relying on his wife to guide him through parenthood and the raising of children. She had been loving, kind, and affectionate and had the sweetest disposition. He fell in love with her precisely because he believed she would make a wonderful mother for his children. So when she died, Jacob wasn't only shattered, he was completely out of his depth. He had no idea how to be a parent. He only knew that he *must* be one. And to him that meant he must keep the boy safe, fed, clothed, and guided in the ways of the Lord. Jacob was always patient with the boy. He never raised his hand to him or otherwise caused his son any harm. Normie would find it hard to find fault with his father, for Jacob was fair, kind, and judicious. But nevertheless, Normie spent his childhood longing for something more. He wanted a family. He had but one dream: a large, noisy, fun-filled, and affectionate family.

By the time Normie was eighteen years old, Jacob presented his son with a sizable amount of money for his son's education.

"I've been putting a little aside for years now. It's enough to send you to England, so you too can go to divinity school. Like my father helped me, I can help you," Jacob said solemnly, if not a bit proud of himself for making such an overt gesture.

"Father," Normie began. He swallowed, his throat suddenly dry as bones. "I can't accept this. I mean, what I mean to say is— well, I don't *want* this."

"What do you mean? We have talked about this for years! You've always dreamed of going to England. I've told you stories of how beautiful it is there and how wonderful it is to study there . . ."

"Father, that was *your* dream," Normie said quietly.

"Excuse me? I thought . . ." Jacob stopped himself and began to search his own memories of past conversations. Normie watched as the truth slowly occurred to Jacob: *It had been he and only he, Jacob, who had ever spoken of Normie going to England.*

"Why didn't you stop me? Why didn't you tell me this earlier, son?" Jacob pleaded.

"I didn't want to disappoint you. I didn't want to break your heart or have you think that I was ungrateful," Normie said quietly.

"Ungrateful? Why would I ever think that of my own son?" Jacob asked.

"You gave so much to me. You raised me all on your own. I know it couldn't have been easy," Normie said.

"You have a good heart, son," Jacob said, nodding. After looking out the window for some long, quiet moments as he was wont to do, Jacob's attention refocused. "So what is it that you want to do? Do you want to go to a nearby university?"

"I'd like to be a farmer like your brother James and like your father before him. Actually, I'd like to have a large apple orchard. And I'd like to have about fifteen kids of my own to help me on it!" Normie said excitedly, simply dreaming of the prospect of a future he had longed for his entire life.

Jacob's eyes widened in shock. It was everything he had longed to get away from as a child—the noise, the uncertainty, the hard work. "You can't be serious?" Jacob asked, laughing. "Fifteen children? Apples? Really? This is what you want?"

"I do. I'd like to go live with Uncle James on your father's homestead for a while—get to know farming a bit. I'd like to buy some land of my own, marry a nice girl, and start a family right away," Normie said excitedly, having given this a great deal of thought.

"And am I to assume that this *nice girl* you intend on marrying is your friend Edna Farr—the girl from school and the socials?"

"Yes, father," Normie said, smiling. "I'd like to marry her soon."

Jacob nodded his head and scanned their spartan living room. "I don't have much to offer you both in terms of heirlooms or a place to get started." Jacob smiled.

"It doesn't matter to us. I'll find work until I save enough to buy some land."

"A man and the land." Jacob shook his head. "It's as if it runs in my family's veins—this need to own their own land and this desire to be fruitful and multiply."

"It does appear that way, though it seems to have skipped a generation, no?" Normie cracked a smile.

"I said something similar to my own father so many years ago," Jacob replied. "He was so kind and generous, and even though I am sure it broke his heart that I chose a different path than his, he never let me know it. In fact, he paid for my passage to England so that I would be able to live my dreams. And now I want to do the same for you."

"What do you mean, Father?"

"Take the money I intended for you to use for school and buy some land for you and Edna."

"Father, I couldn't . . ."

"You can and you will. It will be a great honor, and it will be a way I can repay my own father in a way for the generosity he bestowed on to me. Each generation owes the last. And the best way to pay them back is to give to the next. So that's what I intend to do."

Normie wanted to hug his father, he wanted to embrace him with all his might, but he realized he might crush the man if he did. His father was so frail and small-boned. So unlike him in every way. Instead of such an overt gesture, Normie put out his hand to shake his father's. His father, in a rare and surprising move, swatted his son's hand away and reached out to embrace him instead.

Normie melted into the embrace. For the first time in his life he felt his father's arms wrapped firmly around him. Much taller than the older man, Normie's head bent down to rest on his father's shoulder. He could smell the shaving lather he used and a faint hint of peppermint. He didn't want to leave. He felt so safe and so loved. *Why was it that in life*, Normie wondered, *that just when you felt safe, life had a way of pushing you forward out of that comfort?* It was time for him to grow up, move on, and become a man of his own. But he wondered again: *Does a man ever lose the longing for his father's embrace? Does he ever lose the desire to be his father's son?* Tears rolled gently down Normie's face. He made a solemn vow to himself that when the time would come for his own children to choose their own paths in life, he would be as noble, gracious, and generous as his own father had been to him. He would pay back the last generation by giving to the next. He was certain of it. He'd bet his life on it.

• • •

Normie made his father proud. In short order, he and Edna married and purchased a large orchard from an elderly couple who had run a successful cider mill for more than three decades. In no time at all, Normie, who was now going by *Norm*, was turning a profit and planting even more trees, ensuring the success of future generations as well. All of his childhood dreams were working out but for one. After three pregnancies, poor Edna had yet been unable to give birth to a healthy child. The first two ended in late miscarriages, and the last child died during a long and painful labor. Norm was undeterred, certain that the Lord would reward him and Edna with enough healthy children to run an orchard—and so he and Edna kneeled together beside each other and prayed for the conception of a healthy child before they climbed into bed each night.

Norm adored his wife, and it pained him to see her suffer. Knowing how terribly guilty she felt for not being able to carry a child to term, Norm blamed himself and believed it was because she was working too hard and was under too much pressure. And so after the death of their third baby, he refused to let her help in the orchards any longer, hiring a maid to help her with the housekeeping. He doted on Edna and made sure she wanted for nothing. He would go to the ends of the earth, he promised her, to make her happy.

When their first healthy son finally came, on the four-year anniversary of their wedding, they named the boy Jacob after Norm's beloved father. They adored the baby, who arrived on a fall day right in the middle of one of their most successful and abundant harvests in September of 1875. They believed his birth and the harvest foretold a bright and abundant future. Norm was well on his way to creating the family he had always dreamed about.

But, their joy was short lived. Tragedy soon befell them again. For the next three years, Edna experienced a series of miscarriages. It strained their marriage, and Norm began to worry about his wife's health. She, however, had other concerns.

"Would you be upset with me, Norm, if all I can give you is one son? If all we have is Jacob? Would that be enough for you?" Edna asked her husband one day, weeping in a moment of sheer grief after the miscarriage of a sixth child. "I know you dream of having a house full of children! What if I can't give you your dream? Will you resent me forever? Will you hate me?"

"Of course I wouldn't be upset! Oh, my goodness. That's why you think I am sad? Because we do not yet have more children?" Norm asked. "My dear, I am only concerned about you. I worry day and night about what this is doing to you. My only desire is for your health and happiness! And I love Jacob. We are a happy family. If the Lord desires us to be a small, happy family, then it is his will." Norm kissed his wife on the forehead.

The Lord made his will known in time. Between 1879 and 1892, and in quick succession, Edna had six more children—Clara; Archibald "Archie"; Rebecca; Mary Charlotte; Norman Jr. "Normie"; Nellie; and finally the baby of the family, Robert, or "Bobby."

Those were happy years.

Norm spent his days in the orchard with the older children, while Edna stayed inside tending to the younger ones, cooking, sewing, and creating a warm and happy home for them all. During the long winter months, she homeschooled the children and taught them how to read, write, and play the piano.

"I have been so blessed and lucky!" Norm would often exclaim, sitting across from Enda at their long dinner table. To the right and to the left, chairs all around the table were filled with children. And they adored each of them. As the years went by, the children grew up to be strong and smart. The older girls, Clara, Rebecca, and Mary Charlotte, though not beautiful or extraordinary in any particular way, nevertheless had suitors lined up outside Norm's door. They were all social and chatty and knew how to work a room. Though preoccupied with finding suitors, they were nevertheless devoted to their mother when they were home. The girls never wanted to cause her worry or harm, so they did their best to obey her and help her with the household chores. Only one of them had a little fire in them, and that was the youngest of the girls, Nellie. But because she was sweet, charming, and beautiful, Norm never felt the desire to reprimand her. He couldn't bring himself to do it. Young Nellie was his prize—his pride and joy. She was a small, sweet child with an angelic face and a disposition that reflected her countenance. She was jovial and kind-hearted—but fierce. When she was just a little girl, she carried a tiny doll around with her everywhere. Once Norm tried to take it from her when it was time for bed. She clung to the doll desperately and smacked her father's hand for trying to take it from her. Norm had to hold back the laughter as he watched the little girl's face grow hot with rage.

"She's mine! You can't take her!" Nellie shouted.

Norm, regaining his composure, put on a stern expression. "Now Nellie! It's your bedtime! I won't take this disobedience."

"Well, I won't take *you* taking my doll!" she shouted back.

Norm broke with laughter. She was too sweet and earnest for him to be angry with. But he could see a fire in her at a young age, a willingness to defy him that none of his other girls had.

By the time the baby, Bobby, the last of their children came along, Nellie had fully adopted him as yet another one of her dolls. She doted on him and loved him. Should any other sibling come to play or tickle him, she would swat them away.

"Mine! He's mine! He's my baby bru-dder," she would shout.

Everyone found it adorable and let Nellie play mother to her little brother, "Bobbert." Perhaps no one loved it more than Edna, who appreciated the help. It wasn't every day a toddler was so willing to assist with minding the baby. She could count on Nellie to sit by the cradle and rock it gently or hold a bottle for the little one, too.

"Such a lovely little mother you are to Bobby, Nellie," Edna would say with a smile.

•••

As the two youngest grew up, the eldest children left for college or marriages of their own. Jacob was seventeen years old when Bobby was born, and so by the time Bobby was two, Jacob had already left to attend an engineering school. Clara married and moved out at just eighteen years old. And by the time young Bobby was just seven years old, he was already a young uncle.

One year after Clara married, Archie, the second oldest son, decided he wanted to set off to follow in his grandfather's footsteps and sail for England and divinity school. Norm saw so much of his own father in Archie. Just like his father, Archie was smaller in stature and preferred to be indoors and reading.

As Archie had never much shown an affinity for hard labor or the outdoors, Norm did harbor suspicions of laziness, as much as he loved his son. So when one day Archie couldn't get out of bed, Norm's first reaction was anger.

"You can't just lie about in bed all day! Get up! Get up!"

Archie apologized. "I am sorry. I want to, Father, but my legs won't move."

"What do you mean your legs won't move? Who's ever heard of such a thing! Move them!" Norm shouted.

"I can't," Archie said, panic rising in his voice.

Edna rushed to the boy and felt his head. "He's burning up. We need a doctor! Go get a doctor, Norm!" Edna shouted.

The shouts roused the house, and the other children ran to Archie's room. Among them were ten-year-old Nellie and eight-year-old Bobby.

"What's happening to him, Mama?" Nellie asked.

"He's sick, darling. Now run along and take your little brother with you. I don't want you both catching what he has. All of you, run along outside! Go!" Edna urged, pushing them off and turning her attention back to Archie.

Over the next two nights, Archie's fever showed no signs of breaking. Edna and Norm took shifts watching him and applying cool washcloths to his head.

The doctor didn't know what afflicted the boy, only that he had heard of other cases of paralysis in the legs and that it was accompanied by a fever. That it must be some sort of infection was the only clarity he could offer them.

"Is there anything you can do for him? Please?" Edna begged the doctor.

"Watch and pray," the doctor advised.

By the third night, Archie had stopped taking liquids. He was delirious and having hallucinations.

"The angels are coming for me, Father," Archie whispered. "They're all around. Aren't they beautiful? Grandpa was right. Angels are all around us."

Norm could feel an ache rise through his chest. With it he felt a fear he had never known before, even in the darkest days when Edna had lost so many babes. This was different than losing a baby. He had *loved* Archie. He had bounced him on his knee. He had taken his son's hand in his and walked him and up and down the orchard. He had flung the boy up on his shoulders to pick apples and felt the fat pads of his chubby baby hands squeeze his cheeks. He felt his son's head bend over his so their cheeks would touch. Norm had grown up without affection and wouldn't let his own children's experience be the same. He had relished these moments—moments like holding his son under the golden autumn light.

Later, as he had watched the boy grow, he listened to him expound on the Scriptures with the same brilliance and introspection as his own father had. During the holidays, he loved to hear the boy sing Christmas carols with his sisters around the piano in the parlor. When the boy became a teenager, Norm had looked on in pride as his son square danced with pretty girls under the lights at the annual harvest ball. He was such a handsome young man, and a brilliant one, too. He was there when his son received his letter of acceptance to divinity school. He felt the pride only a father can feel for watching a son become a man before his eyes. And now he was watching as his son transitioned from this life to the next. It was unfathomable. He could not endure this. He could not say goodbye to a child he loved and cared for with all his heart and soul. *What a world! What a world*, he cried to himself. *To lose a boy such as this!*

As he heard Archie gasp and struggle for air, he knew the time was coming. He quickly shot up to wake Edna, who had fallen asleep. "Edna—Edna, dear, it's time." Without speaking, Edna knew, as all mothers know. She sat beside her son on his bed and took his hand in hers and silently sang his favorite hymn, "Amazing Grace."

Norm looked on in disbelief. *Just last week the boy was alive and well. How can this be happening? How is it that we come to love so much, only to have it snatched away?* Then he thought of his poor wife, the agony she must be in. His heart broke all over again.

Their son was gone. *Gone.* Forever.

• • •

Months later, the once happy McCombs home was still overwhelmed with despair. Edna had taken to her bed. Nellie, always ready to play nursemaid, made it her duty to care for her mother around the clock. Norm, overcome with grief, knew no other way to deal with the grief than to throw himself into his work. If he was in the orchard, he was safe. His mind was busy, and most importantly, he was far from the other children. The sight of the younger ones filled him with dread. He simply could not risk becoming attached to them as he had let himself become to Archie.

The girls saw the change in their father and didn't take his aloofness personally. They had their mother to tend to and their household chores to keep them occupied. But the young boys,

Normie and Bobby, felt their father's sudden coldness toward them acutely. Their father had always asked them to join him in the orchard. They now were instructed to stay at home with their sisters and help their mother. At night when they all gathered for dinner, there was no laughter or lightness in the conversation. Their father showed no interest in their daily activities. He asked them no questions. He ate and simply retired to his bedroom each night, bringing a bowl of soup up to his wife, who refused to leave the bedroom.

The children who remained in the house learned quickly that they must fend for themselves. Each child found new ways to survive under these circumstances. Normie, who was eleven when his brother Archie died, wanted desperately to please his father. He tried to be a good son and not cause any trouble. Bobby, on the other hand, was desperate for attention and acted out. He would gladly take being reprimanded by his father over being ignored by him. The one person who had shown him any attention, Nellie, was now preoccupied caring for their mother. He was utterly alone. No mother. No father. No friends. As the darkness set over the home, Bobby wanted nothing more than to escape the palpable sadness that enveloped them all. He wanted to get as far away from the farm and the memories of his older, beloved brother and the happy life they had all once shared.

Norm, on the other hand, wanted the impossible. He wanted to go back in time. He wanted to return to those happy days when all of his children were at home safe and sure in the knowledge that they were loved. His entire life he had worked to create a family, a legacy, and now all he could do was watch as one by one each child left him—to marriage, to schools, to death. Loneliness creeped in, the depths of which he was not aware existed, and grief overwhelmed his days. All of his dreams, all of his hopes had been buried on a hill that he could see from his bedroom window.

Someday his wife would die too and join Archie and all the babies they had lost. Someday he would as well, and then and only then, he would have some peace. But on this day, the only day he had or could bring himself to think about, he felt that it was an enormous heartbreak to be alive.

11

It All Came Out So Wrong

uzy could tell something was bothering Douglas. Though often demonstrative and forthcoming, he had a tendency to withdraw from her on occasion. She attributed this to him missing his late wife. Suzy knew that no matter how much he professed to love her, he couldn't help but mourn and miss his wife. After all, they had spent a lifetime together. It never bothered her when she saw him retreat into himself. She understood. She knew what it was like to love someone and care deeply for someone for a long time. She also knew what it was like to remember the bad memories as well as the good. And she also knew how complicated it was to love an imperfect person in an imperfect relationship. She knew that as humans, we want desperately to only remember the good, which, ironically, can make moving on so hard. She knew well that it was remembering the difficult times, the times that nearly broke her, that were the times that helped her heal the most. Because the difficult times allowed her to forgive herself and, in turn, her ex-husband and move on.

There were things she didn't tell Douglas. He was protective. He had a fight in him. She knew that if she brought certain things up, they would only make him angry—not at her, of course, but at her ex. She didn't want Douglas to be angry. She was done with anger and conflict. Suzy had spent her entire life fighting for a moment's peace—first with her mother, then her ex, and she wasn't about to spend the rest of her life repeating the same loop over and over. She liked her peaceful life, her routine, her job, friends, dancing. She liked being with Douglas. He made her laugh. He took care of her every need. The past was in the past. There was no need to dredge it up—not in her, and not in him. So if he wanted to take a long walk or spend a day or two away from her, she understood. She never asked why, and she didn't need to, because she trusted him. She trusted his heart.

Suzy could hear him. He'd been up all night pacing the floor. Something was eating away at him. He often spiraled like this. He couldn't get ahead of the thoughts that consumed him. She understood this is what made him brilliant—he had the ability to continue to think through a problem until he found the optimum solution—but it was also his downfall. Some things, Suzy knew, one simply couldn't know. Unlike Douglas, she had learned to make peace with the unknown. She had learned to let go and forgive. This is how she survived, how she woke up every morning with a smile. This is how she was able to make it through all those lonely, hard days on her own, after her husband left her.

And that was the truth of it. *Her husband had* left her. Suzy was well aware that when she told Douglas about her past, she had been purposely vague. She'd never lied; she had merely said they were ill-suited. She had said he was controlling and that she'd felt hopeless—all of these were true statements. But what she left out was what she could not bring herself to say aloud. It hurt, still, after all these years to speak the truth of it. She had not left him first. She hadn't had the courage to stand up to him. She felt shame over this. And she didn't want Douglas's pity—or his anger. She wanted it— whatever *it* was—to remain hers and hers alone. The truth was she wanted to have children. She was desperate to have children. And her husband had been too, but she couldn't get pregnant. She had tried and tried. She thought it was a failure on her part, and that her husband's anger and resentment toward her were well-deserved.

The one thing they both wanted desperately, she simply could not do, and her ex-husband wanted no part of adoption or any other methods.

As the years went by and friends of theirs had children, the absence of their own became more prominent, and the chasm between the two grew. He resented her, and in turn she wanted desperately to please him. When he finally took off and didn't return, only calling months later to say he was selling the house and that she had to move, she didn't argue with him. She didn't try to dissuade him. She would have left herself too, Suzy thought, at her lowest moments. She felt as though she had nothing left to give, so it made sense that he should take it all.

But Suzy knew Douglas well. He paid the checks at restaurants, held the door for her, walked her home from work, spoke with her about "arrangements" should anything happen to him. He was the type of man who took care of the people in his life. She knew Douglas simply couldn't fathom a man who could leave his spouse destitute, homeless, and for a reason so unthinkable—an act she had no control over her ability to perform: carrying a child.

Those were things in the past, things best not said. They were things she couldn't speak—not to him, not to anyone.

Some burdens are best carried alone.

Suzy didn't expect Douglas to return for the day. She had heard the door slam sometime past seven a.m. He had come back to the room shortly before that time to gather his things. She pretended to be asleep, because she knew he needed a break. She wasn't worried that he would never return. She wasn't the type of person who carried her old hurts from past lovers and projected them on to new ones. She knew that Douglas was a keeper. She knew he would never harm her or willingly leave her. She knew he was a man who sometimes needed time to be alone and grieve.

So when he arrived shortly after nine a.m. with coffee, pastries, and the newspaper, she was startled.

"You're back!"

"Of course. I wouldn't just leave without telling you," Douglas said, setting down the coffees on the table and laying out the newspaper. "It's a nice day. I thought we could walk to Midtown and catch a play. Here," he said, pushing the paper over to her. "Pick one out."

"Oh, Douglas," she said, laughing at herself.

"What?" he asked, confused. "What did I do that's so funny?"

"You had me worried. You were up all night and pacing. I thought that you needed one of your breaks," she said quietly.

"One of my breaks?" Douglas said as if surprised by the revelation.

"You know, when you get sad—and you want to remember Hope. I understand. It doesn't bother me."

Douglas looked at her and smiled. "Actually, I was up all night thinking about *you*."

"Me? Why me?"

"Something you said yesterday I couldn't get out of my mind," he said.

"Oh," Suzy said quietly.

"Oh," Douglas repeated. "So there is something you're not telling me?"

"What's this all about, Douglas? Where's this coming from?" she asked with a laugh, gently nudging him.

"I don't know, I just sensed that you were withholding something from me. I can always tell when someone is holding something back. And, I can't help it. My mind won't let it go. I love you so much. I know you know that. And there is nothing you could tell or say to me that would make me love you any less."

"I know that, Douglas."

"Then what is it you're not telling me?" he asked.

"Well, I could be asking you the same thing," she replied.

"What?" Douglas asked. "What do you mean by that?"

"It just seems to me that if you're so sure I'm holding something back, it must be because you're holding something back as well," she said forcefully. "Besides, everyone holds stuff back. That's how the world operates! We can't all just blab everything we think and feel out to the world. It would be absolute chaos. Some things are best left unsaid. Let's just leave it be. I won't ask you what you're holding back, if you don't ask me," she said, slipping on her readers and opening the paper to let Douglas know the conversation was over.

"No," Douglas said.

"No?" Suzy looked up. "No, what?"

"No, I don't buy it. I don't believe that. I think when two people are together they should be open with each other. They should be able to bare their souls. They should be able to say the things they can't say to anyone else."

Suzy took off her readers and leaned over and took his hand, "Okay, Douglas, tell me what's on your mind. Tell me your secret. I am here. I am listening."

"No, no, no," he said, pulling his hand away and laughing. "I see what you're doing! You're going to get me to start talking and you know I won't stop. And then you won't tell me what you're keeping from me!"

"What I am keeping from you!" Suzy chortled. "And what may I ask in that brilliant mind of yours do you think I am keeping from you?"

"I have no idea! That's why I am asking you!"

"I don't know what you want me to say, Douglas. I don't know what you're looking for from me. I don't know any other way to be than this. This is who I am. I don't have a lot of secrets. I don't have any hang-ups or resentments. I am a happy person. I like my life. I feel like you're making me look for problems."

"I'm not. I'm sincerely not. If you don't have anything to say, then I'll stop. You're right. I am letting my imagination get the best of me. I suppose all this reading about my relatives and all the secrets of the past, I have made some foregone conclusions about humanity in general."

"Like?"

"Like all people have something heartbreaking in their past that they have to survive! Some people have things, impossibly difficult things that they have to live with. Not one of us gets out of this gig alive. And not one of us gets through life without pain or heartbreak," he explained. "I see you—how amazing you are. I see how bright and positive you are, and I am amazed. I wonder: *How did I get so lucky to find someone like her?* And then I think about you and the path you took to find me. And, I may be wrong, but I can see it in your eyes, there's something there. Some pain that you're not telling me. And I just wish you could know that no matter what's in your heart—no matter how big the break—I can take it. I won't even try to fix it. I know that's impossible, but I want to be there for you. That's all." Douglas quietly took her hand.

Suzy lifted his hand to her cheek and held it. She closed her eyes and stayed quiet for a long time before she broke the silence between them.

"I didn't leave him," she said quietly.

Douglas looked shocked and pulled his hand away, thinking that she was telling him something else . . . that perhaps she was still with him.

"No, no, no, don't get the wrong idea, Douglas," she said, recognizing his confusion.

"We're divorced. But he was the one who divorced me. I know I made it sound like we were in a difficult marriage and I was the one who left. But in truth, he left me," she said quietly. "I probably would have remained in that unhappy and miserable marriage for years if he hadn't made the first move. And I guess that's why I am so grateful. It's why I forgive him for all he did," she said.

"What did he do to you, Suzy?"

"He didn't abuse me, if that's what you're wondering. Not physically. But he left me because—" Suzy held her breath. This was harder than she ever thought possible to say.

"What? You can tell me, Suzy. Just tell me," Douglas asked.

"I couldn't have children. I *can't* have children. I tried everything. But nothing worked. I felt like a failure. I felt like I let us down. In the end, he couldn't even look at me. He moved. Sold the house out from under me, and left me with nothing," Suzy said.

"My God," Douglas said, his face becoming red with rage.

"Now see, I didn't want you to get angry. I knew you would be upset. I'm not upset anymore, Douglas. I made peace with this a long time ago. His leaving me was the best thing that ever happened to me. I would have never had the courage to do it. I would have stayed and been miserable. And I would have never met you and, of course, I would have never started the process—" Suzy broke off as soon she realized she'd said too much.

"Started what process?" Douglas asked.

Suzy hesitated and got up. "Well, we really should start getting ready if we want to make to a matinee."

"I don't want to go to a play, Suzy. *Started what?*"

Suzy turned and looked at him. "Before I met you. Before we started to date, I—I—I—I was going to tell you. Eventually, if it turned out . . ."

"Tell me *what?*" Douglas said, getting nervous—though he wasn't sure why. Suddenly he felt nauseated; a wave washed over him. The thought of losing her, the thought of something coming between them, terrified him.

"I've started the process of adopting. I am only fifty. I have a lot of life in me. I realized a long time ago, I can still be a mother if I wanted to. My ex never entertained adoption as an option. But I don't care whether I have the baby myself or not.

I don't care about genes or where a child comes from. I just want to be a mother. I can be a mother. And I know I'd be a wonderful one. And there are plenty of children out there who need a mother."

A brief wave of relief washed over Douglas. *Adoption! A child? She wants a child?* "So this is what you've been keeping from me! Why didn't you tell me any of this? How far along in the process are you?" Douglas asked.

"Pretty far. At first, I didn't know where you and I were headed. And if I apply as a single person, I have a good shot at it happening soon. If I were to bring a boyfriend, partner, or spouse into it, it could slow things down. They would have to be investigated too, and I wasn't sure if you would even want to . . . or how to ask . . ." Suzy said, fumbling.

"I can't get married," Douglas said out loud, shocking even himself with the revelation.

"Okay," Suzy said quietly, feeling a chill come between them. "I wasn't asking you to. I wouldn't even presume . . ."

"What I mean is, I can't go through that again," Douglas said. "I can't marry someone, love them, and lose them . . . I just can't." Douglas became agitated, though he couldn't explain why.

"I am not asking you to marry me, Douglas, or to be on this journey with me. I don't need you to help me adopt. If that's what you're worried about. You don't have to feel obligated . . ."

"When were you going to tell me this?" Douglas asked. "When were you going to tell me? When the baby came? When the phone call came that a baby was ready? *When?*"

"I don't know," Suzy said, standing up and walking out of the kitchen.

"Where are you going?" Douglas said.

"I need to get some fresh air," Suzy said, grabbing her jacket and putting it on.

Douglas got up from the chair quickly. He felt lightheaded. His blood pressure had fallen. This had been happening lately, especially when he got upset or his heart began to race. It was as if his heart couldn't keep up.

Watching her leave set him into a panic. He hadn't meant to say those things. Everything was happening so fast. He had just been caught off guard. He didn't want her to leave. He didn't want her thinking he didn't want a child, or that he didn't want to be with her. *It all came out so wrong.* All of it was just such a shock.

When he heard the door open, he rushed toward it.

The last thing Douglas remembered was seeing Suzy descend the concrete stairs that led out to the city street. He had tried to reach out to stop her. He saw his hand go toward hers and then the world fell away. It became a black abyss into which he fell.

• • •

What Douglas didn't see was that just as he passed out at the top of the stairs, his body heaved forward and fell heavily, taking Suzy, only a couple of steps below, down with him. The two tumbled down the concrete stairs together. When they finally hit the bottom, Suzy's clavicle snapped on impact, and her whole body felt the weight of Douglas's as he landed on her.

Despite the crushing pain, she was conscious and able to slide out from underneath him. Confused for a moment, she sat up and dragged herself up toward Douglas's face to see if he was breathing. That's when she noticed the blood pooling on the pavement. A wave of horror washed over her. Suzy hesitated to look, but knew she must. She reached over to examine the source of the blood and saw that the back of Douglas's head was split, a massive gash bisecting the back of his skull.

"Oh, Douglas! No!"

12

ROBERT "BOBBY"/"MAC" McCOMBS

Partnered with Gladys McCombs, and Father of Robert, Edna, Gladys, and Douglas

---

Born April 18, 1892, in Moulton Township, Haldimand Co., Ontario
Died (1967, Buffalo, New York)
Son of Norman McCombs and Edna Sephronia Farr
Brother of Jacob, Clara, Archibald, Rebecca,
Mary Charlotte, Norman, and Nellie
Grandson of Rev. Jacob McCombs and
Mary Ann (Bessey) McCombs
Married to Margaret Ott, Father of Ruth McCombs

*R*obert "Bobby" McCombs was a dreamer. For most of his childhood, he ran freely and happily in his father's orchard. There among the trees, he and his brother Normie and sister Nellie would play for hours. They imagined all sorts of things that young children do. They climbed trees and pretended to be high up on the masts of old sailing vessels. Nothing seemed impossible to Bobby then. Sitting high up in the trees, he looked out over his father's land and imagined what it would be like to travel far beyond it. Like many young boys, he longed for adventure, travel, and far-off lands. When he was young, Bobby's father entertained and encouraged these dreams.

"You can do anything you put your mind to, Bobby. With hard work and determination, you can achieve anything," Norm would tell him, as his own father had told him. Bobby was nothing if not a hard worker. Unlike most dreamers—Bobby had a strong sense of doing, too. He followed his father around, learning everything he could about running a farm. His older brother was a skilled carpenter, and Bobby apprenticed with him as well. As a boy, he picked things up quickly. Adept at math, he could run numbers in his head quickly and with accuracy. At dinner, his father would list numbers and ask Bobby to add them at lightning speed. It was almost a party trick. He was so quick that he would come up with the answer—before his own father could—using a pencil and paper to do the arithmetic. Though his father never said it, he was so proud of his brilliant son.

Bobby was adored by his mother and older sisters, too. Perhaps no one adored him more than his sister Nellie, who showered him with affection from the day he was born. There was no lack of love or support in those early years, and it was a good thing too— for that foundation would sustain him during the long, painful years that came later after the death of his brother Archie.

Bobby's father never recovered from the death of Archie.

Normie and Bobby were just boys then. Bobby was only about eight years old. It was the turning point in his life. His father's demeanor changed overnight. He no longer wanted his sons around. He no longer asked Bobby to do math problems at the dinner table. He no longer smiled at the boys. Bobby took it personally. The boy didn't understand grief. He didn't understand depression. Of course, there were no words for such a thing back then. All he knew was that his father no longer spoke to him or looked at him. Young Bobby felt ignored and unmoored. He became, like so many neglected children, angry and resentful. Watching his weary father walk slowly up and down the orchard now repulsed him. He thought of his father as lazy, pathetic, and sad. Sitting across from his sullen father at dinner enraged young Bobby. He wanted an escape from the depths of this negativity.

Bobby had dreams, and he didn't care what it took to achieve them. He would work—day and night if he had to. He wanted to run his own farm someday—a dairy. He loved animals and wanted to be surrounded by them—cows, cats, dogs—it didn't matter. He wanted his life to be teeming with *life*—living things, a family, animals, adventure, and success. He loved the liveliness of his early childhood and longed to return to it or at least create a new and better version of it.

As soon as he came of working age, Bobby worked alongside his older brother in his barn-building business. He became an adept carpenter. He also worked in a knitting mill—earning as much money as he could stash away and save so that he could one day purchase his own dairy. He also attended a business school. He knew he would need certain skills to help run a successful business, and he didn't want to overlook any aspect. He had only three goals: To be a success. To be happy. To be totally different from his own father.

Like many sons, Bobby's resistance to his father informed his life choices. He threw himself into work and love and found every means to rebel against what he saw as his father's failure and weakness.

When he met a beautiful girl, Margaret, a Catholic who his father would never approve of, he asked her to marry him almost immediately. He couldn't say it was because of love exactly—more as a means of escape. The sooner he was married with a family of his own, the sooner he could get away from the father and home he so despised.

"If you marry a Catholic—outside our church, your grandfather's church—you can't expect your mother and I to be there—to support a Papist," his father said sullenly.

"As if I care what you think," Bobby retorted. His patience for his father had by then run thin. Bobby was in his early twenties—and had a sizeable nest egg of his own. He could do anything he wished—leave, marry a Catholic, it didn't matter. Besides, no matter what he did, he never got a reaction out of his father either way. If he had married a good Protestant girl and decided to stay on the orchard, his father wouldn't so much have said, "Congratulations!" so in Bobby's mind, leaving was no different.

"If you go through with this, you'll no longer be welcome here. Do you understand me?"

"Perfectly," Bobby said. His bags were already packed.

In short order, Bobby married the Catholic girl, Margaret Ott, and a daughter, Ruth, soon followed.

Bobby worked day and night—saving as much money as he could to eventually buy a dairy and go into business on his own.

He scoured the papers daily looking for land and the perfect place to settle down with his wife and daughter. When he read about a dairy being sold across the border in the U.S., he wasted no time. This was his chance. He too could build a business, be successful, and live the life he always wanted. In 1917, he packed his family up and moved to the United States. This was a new start for the McCombses—a whole new line of American McCombses.

By 1921, Bobby had everything he ever wanted. He had a wife, a daughter, and a dairy. He owned dogs and cats. People in the community knew him by name, "Mac." And his name was easy to remember. After all, "McCombs" was engraved on every milk bottle in the county. Life as he knew it could not be any better.

For the better part of ten years, Mac worked around the clock to build his business. He was a bit of a risk taker, and when he heard about some stocks that were sure to bring about a huge return, Mac quickly ran the numbers and saw gold. He and his wife would be rich—the richest people in the county. In order to buy the stocks, he had to take out another mortgage on the dairy. *Not a problem*, he thought. *The returns on the stocks will invariably pay the mortgage off and then some.*

When Mac opened the paper one morning in early 1927, his face blanched. Two years before the official stock market crash, he faced a personal crash. While everyone else was getting rich, Mac had chosen poorly. All the blood drained from his face. He suddenly felt like he had swallowed a large pill and it had gotten caught in his throat. He looked at the stock he had invested his life's fortune in—it was obliterated. *He* was obliterated. He would lose the dairy. His home. All of his dreams. In one day, everything he had worked for, everything he had bet his future on had been blown up. In a word: devastating.

He collapsed on the front porch. He thought of suicide. For a brief moment the idea of killing himself flashed before his eyes. He could end all of it—the shame that would surely follow— if he just ended his life right then and there. Then he thought of his daughter, Ruth, without a father. He thought of his wife, Margaret—a Catholic. The shame she would endure. He would not even be allowed a proper burial.

There was no way out of this. He had to face his mistake like a man—with courage. He had to tell his wife what he had done. He had to figure out a way out of this mess. He had worked hard before. He knew how to work. He would fix this, he thought.

When he walked into the kitchen, Margaret was frying eggs for breakfast. He took a moment to look at her from behind. To capture the moment, this one last time she would know security, peace, and happiness. What he was about to tell her would destroy all of that. It would not only destroy his dreams—but hers as well. She wanted the same things as him—freedom, wealth, prosperity. She wanted a bigger house someday, fine clothes, and jewelry. She talked endlessly about her dreams—wanting lavish vacations aboard ships that would take them across the sea and entertaining the locals with dinner parties and events.

When he broke the news, Margaret immediately recoiled. She pulled her hand from her husband's. He had tried to be delicate. He had tried to break the news to her softly. He had taken her hand and kissed it as he so often had when they had been courting.

"I wanted more for us. I wanted too much. I am afraid, this time, I risked too much," he whispered.

As he explained what he had done and what position he put the family in, Margaret grew hot with rage. Her disgust and frustration spilled out. In the midst of her tirade, she spoke words that Mac could hardly believe he was hearing.

"I knew it! I knew you would screw this up! You're exactly the failure my father said you were. He warned me about you. He said you would turn out just like your own father—a sad, old pathetic orchard farmer. And look at you now! Look at you! You've destroyed everything. You've ruined everything. We're ruined! How could you have been so foolish? So stupid? I married you for your money, not for your brains or good looks, obviously, and now look what I am left with!"

The words stung Mac. He felt like he had been stabbed in the chest.

Margaret stormed out of the house. Mac sat alone in the kitchen and was numb. Everything he believed had been annihilated in an instant. He had believed optimism would pay off. He believed hope was something one could build a life on. He believed his wife had married him for love. For the first time in his life, he understood his own father. Again, he grew closer to understanding his own father and what it felt like to lose everything one cherished in an instant.

Mac vowed to make things work. He vowed to turn things around. Even as the bank came, just a few months later, to repossess the dairy, Mac swore he would be able to work and provide for Margaret and Ruth. He bought a run-down home in Amherst. It wasn't much; it was no farmhouse. But it would do. Margaret, however, hated it. And she resented having to move, having to raise their daughter in such conditions. Still, Bobby remained hopeful. Even when Margaret and Ruth boarded a train in early 1928 to go back home to her parents in Canada, a year before the stock market crashed and nearly obliterated everyone else in the United States, Mac was still hoping things would turn around. He had taken a job as a day laborer in Buffalo and even boarded freights in Lake Erie to make money. He believed hard work would pay off eventually. Margaret was in no mood for hope.

"Don't bother coming for us. I'll look into an annulment," were the last things he heard his wife say as she disappeared behind the train doors.

• • •

Not long after Margaret boarded the train, another beautiful woman caught Mac's eye. He was walking down a street in

Buffalo when he happened to glance in a beauty shop's window and saw a young woman using a hot iron to marcel another woman's hair into the popular, wavy fashion of the time. She was laughing and talking to the other women in the salon. Something in him made him stop. He couldn't explain what had come over him. It was if he was being tugged—no, pushed—to open the doors of the shop and introduce himself to the young woman. Unable to resist the compulsion, he found himself, hat in hand, standing in the middle of a beauty shop, surrounded by women sitting with their hair pinned and staring at him.

"Excuse me, miss," he said, firmly and resolutely.

"Who, me?" the young hairdresser asked, turning toward him and then looking around behind her to see if he was speaking to someone else.

"Yes, you. What's your name, may I be so bold to ask?" Mac asked.

"Gladys," she said.

"Gladys," he said with a smile. "That's pretty."

She looked startled, almost in shock, about what was transpiring. It was so unexpected and out of the ordinary.

"You're very pretty, Gladys. I was walking down the street, on my way to work, and I was wondering if after your shift—my shift—later tonight, I mean, would it be all right if I—" He stuttered a bit and became red in the face.

"All right if you *what*?" Gladys asked.

"All right if I came by and took you out for dinner. Just at the diner over there," he said, pointing across the street.

"I don't even know your name," Gladys responded.

"Robert McCombs. Everyone calls me Mac," he said, walking over to introduce himself. He meant to shake her hand, but when she put her hand out to shake it, he bent over and kissed it. It felt like the most natural thing in the world to do.

Gladys and all the women in the shop stopped and stared. Mac could feel it and pulled away.

"Does six work?" Gladys said.

"Six is fine," Mac said with a smile. "I'll come by and get you."

"All right then," Gladys said, turning back to her customer's hair, pulling out the pins to reveal undulating waves of hair.

"All right, then," Mac said, backing up out of the shop and trying to ignore the giggles and chortles of the other women.

• • •

Gladys and Mac had a whirlwind romance. Neither had money, so neither had anything but the desire to be with each other and enjoy the simple things. Long walks up and down the streets. Nickel movies. Gladys wasn't a dreamer like Mac. She was grounded, a hard worker, and didn't expect much out of life— or Mac. She was a realist, through and through, and Bobby liked that about her. He'd had his heart broken by a dreamer like him. Margaret had crushed him, and he never wanted to feel that way again. She had taken his pride. Worst of all, she had taken their daughter away from him. He had nothing left to live for until he met Gladys. Gladys made him—he often joked—*glad*. He could be himself with her. Moreover, he could count on her.

When she told him she was pregnant, Mac was at once thrilled and panicked at the same time. He couldn't possibly marry her without having received an annulment or divorce from Margaret. *And Gladys didn't even know about Margaret or Ruth.* It hadn't come up. He had tried to forget that part of his history. He was too ashamed of how his marriage ended, and he didn't want it tainting what Gladys would think of him. He couldn't risk telling her the truth and losing her.

"I can't marry you," Mac said immediately.

"Whaddya mean you can't marry me? I am pregnant! I'm having our baby! You said you loved me. You *have* to marry me!" Gladys, ever the realist, laid down the law.

"I can't—*legally*—marry you," Mac admitted.

"Why not?"

"I'm still married to someone else," Mac said quietly.

Gladys recoiled. She pulled away from him. Bobby panicked. He had seen this move before. "It's not what you think!" he blurted out. "*She left me*. Took our daughter back to Canada to live with her parents," he said.

"*Your daughter?* You already have a kid?"

"I do. Her name is Ruth. She's about nine by now. I don't see her. Well, I should say, I don't get to see her. My wife took her from me," he said.

"Why? What did you do? Did you beat them? Cheat on your wife?" Gladys asked, matter of fact.

"No, it was nothing like that."

"Then what? Out with it!" Gladys demanded, putting her hands on her hips.

"I used to run a dairy. I made a bad business decision. I took all the equity out of our house and business and put it all in one stock that went belly up. Friends of mine said it would make me a rich man. I lost everything—including my wife. She didn't take to being a day laborer's wife," he said.

"I see," Gladys said, softening. Then she stared off in the distance as if thinking through things carefully. "So if you're married, *technically*, and the wife lives in Canada, and no one knows this 'round here, suppose we move off into the country somewhere? Build something of our own. Tell people we're married, even though we aren't. Who's gonna know? Who's gonna question it?"

Mac smiled. He liked the way she thought.

"I love you, Mac. I think you've got a good heart. You work hard. You're honest, for the most part, when you're not keeping things from me, that is," she added. "But, as long as you promise me you'll never do that again, I'll stay with you. We can have this baby. We can raise a family of our own. And I don't need to take wedding vows anyhow to promise that I'll stand by you for richer or for poorer. Vows are obviously meaningless. Fat lot of good it did you and your first wife. What I have to offer is better than vows. Better than a marriage. I promise I'll stand by you no matter what life throws at us—good and bad—because that's what love is. It's showing up for each other and sticking by each other. I'll stick by you, Mac McCombs. Because I love you," she said.

Mac felt his heart expand in his chest. He had never loved anyone more in his life than he loved this woman now. Margaret had never made such a promise. She had never declared her love for him in such a way. And if Mac was honest, he needed to *hear* it. He needed to hear that someone loved him. It had been so long since he heard such things. His own parents had withheld affection or any real demonstration of love for years. He had no idea the power of hearing the words "I love you" could have on a person. He wanted to scoop her up in his arms and never let her go.

And that's exactly what he did.

Soon they moved to a spot in the country. He bought three lots for $180, not far from the run-down home he and Margaret once lived in. They had no money, but Mac was resourceful. He gathered scraps of wood and other things most people thought of as garbage and built a small shack. During the day he worked hard for meager pay, as did Gladys, who worked as a cleaning lady at the local theater. They both always seemed to find work; neither ever felt like they were beneath anything. Their main priority was feeding their children—their firstborn, Bobby Jr., and then the girls who soon followed, Edna May and Gladys Mary, and finally the baby of the family, Dougie.

They were poor. Poorer than Mac had hoped to be. He never imagined such a life for himself. Though despite the poverty and struggles, he never lost sight of his dreams. In his mind, he had all that he wanted—dogs, cats, a loving wife, and children. He didn't plan on living in a shack his whole life, and went about building his wife a proper house on the property. After long days at work, he would come home with scraps he had pulled from others' trash, and he began building a larger home on the property—adjacent to the shack. In fact, he built a door between the shack and the new house so that as it was being built, he could move freely from the old home to the new one—and so could the children.

It took him nearly fifteen years to complete from the time he started. The youngest, Dougie, was a teenager by the time he had his own room and could move into the house.

For most of his children's lives, Mac worked. He worked tirelessly and endlessly to put food on the table—and it was never enough. Both he and his wife were terrible with money. They spent it as soon as they got it, and then they never seemed to have it when they needed it.

The children struggled under these circumstances. There was no security—no sense of safety. Perhaps no one felt this more keenly than young Dougie. His mother was forty by the time he was born, his father forty-two. Both were weary by years of intense labor and childrearing, scraping by with little to show for it. As time went on, they had increasingly little energy to expend or attention to give their youngest. Their sole focus was to make enough money to feed everyone. Dreams of grandeur and success had faded into the abyss that is poverty—as living hand to mouth often does. It's hard to have dreams when one can't even sleep.

Though in his youth, Mac resisted his father, Norm, he had a newfound understanding for him as an adult. He knew what it was like to have a dream destroyed. He knew what it was like to watch everything you ever worked and hoped for snuffed out. All his life he was told that with hard work and determination he could achieve anything. But here Mac was at forty-four, father of four (five if he counted Ruth), and all he had to show for all of his hard work was more bills, more endless days of labor ahead of him, with no hope of change on the horizon. It was all he could do to function, let alone show affection toward his own children. Without realizing it, he had become every bit the father to his own children that his own father had been to him—cold, distant, and completely preoccupied with his own suffering.

He had moments, though—fleeting though they were—when he allowed himself to feel something besides sorrow and struggle. When he was asked during World War II to drive a transport vehicle for the army down to Portsmouth, Virginia, he took his young son, Dougie, a toddler then, along with him. It would be impossible for his wife to work with the baby nearby, and it would be a lot easier for Mac to contain the boy in a vehicle and keep an eye on him.

On the trip, Mac tended to the boy. He made sure Dougie ate. He let him sit on his lap and pretend to steer the vehicle. After the vehicle was dropped off, instead of boarding a train back to New York, Mac decided to walk and hitchhike to save the train money and use it toward the home expenses. The walk between Virginia and New York was an arduous one. Often he would have to pick Dougie up and carry him on his shoulders. But Dougie was a good boy and never complained. He liked to pull the boy close, feel his cheek against his, as he often felt his own father's when he was a small boy. When the boy groaned with hunger, Mac found small places to eat and made sure his son ate well before he did—eggs and milk. Sometimes he went without so that his boy could eat.

He didn't have words for it. He couldn't bring himself to say it, but he loved his son. He would do anything for him. He would walk hundreds of miles just to hold him. Just to spend one more day with him. When he thought of his brother Archie, his heart ached for his father. He couldn't imagine ever losing a child, especially one so sweet as dear Dougie. Again, Mac's heart softened for his own father.

As his children grew up in a new and chaotic world that Mac didn't understand, he felt ill-equipped to handle their expectations and their perceptions of him. He didn't need them to point out what a failure he was. *He felt it.* He had spent his entire life working for a dream that was impossible to achieve. He would never be able to become wealthy working for a measly wage around the clock. No man ever had. All he had going for him was his wife Gladys's promise to stand by him, and he her. He had the house he had promised to build her, board by board, window by window. Small and meager though it was, it was his, and he had built it all by himself. It was hardly the type of home his children's friends were living in, but it was a home nonetheless.

It was the fifties, and teenagers now did things he couldn't have fathomed doing at his own age. They wanted cars. They smoked and drank. They ran around with their peers after school and didn't seem to work or have jobs. They listened to "rock n' roll." His oldest son, Bobby Jr., began drinking in high school and was arrested for stealing. He was watched by the police and always getting into trouble—tarnishing what was left of the family's reputation. Worst of all, Bobby Jr. would come home drunk and covered in vomit—disrupting the entire house and making his wife inconsolable. Neither Mac nor his wife knew what to do or how to stop it.

They had worked so hard so their son could have everything.

They gave the boy everything he wanted and all the freedom he himself never had as a child working on the farm. But the boy seemed so ungrateful. He was a handful. All he did was give his mother and father trouble. He tortured their youngest son, Dougie, suffocating him with pillows whenever the opportunity presented itself. Chasing the boy and wrestling him to the ground. It was exhausting trying to manage him—so they didn't. "Boys will be boys," his wife Gladys would say. So they left the two alone. His girls were a mystery to him too. They smoked and drank, though neither Mac nor Gladys smoked or drank. It was unseemly, but the girls said *everyone* did it at school, so their mother and father allowed it. They never went to such schools or understood such things, and so they didn't feel like they could say otherwise.

The only one who didn't bring them any trouble was young Dougie. He was a hard worker. He always seemed to have a job and was ready to help out whenever Mac needed him. He helped with the building of the house. He brought his earnings home and helped keep food on the table. "Dougie never gives us any trouble," was the highest praise they could give a child, and they gave it to Dougie alone.

Dougie needed more than that, though. Like his own father, he longed to hear the words, "I love you." He longed to feel special and wanted. Since he didn't get it at home, he looked elsewhere—at school and then in sports. Dougie hated being at home, surrounded by the squalor. He had dreams too. He had plans to get out of his father's house and make his own way in the world.

When he went to his father to tell him he got into college, Mac balked. "You can't. You can't leave the family," he said.

The thought of losing Dougie was more than he could take. The only thing he had done right in life was Dougie. Dougie didn't drink. Dougie was a hard worker. Dougie thought of other people besides himself. Dougie looked out for his family. Mac's entire life had a been a series of failures and disappointments. Nothing stuck. Nothing had worked out. But Dougie had. Dougie seemed to get what life was about. He was a free thinker and independent. He was strong and a fighter. He had watched his son take on his older brother and defeat him in fights. His son had managed to date the prettiest girl in school, a girl named Hope. Everything Dougie did, Mac was proud of, though he couldn't say it. He didn't have the words for it. He didn't have a template for expressing such emotions. No one had ever said such things to him when he was growing up. So when Dougie asked to go to college, the only answer Bobby could muster was: "No."

Dougie didn't understand; he just wanted out. He wanted to get as far away from the squalor as possible. He didn't see his father as others saw him. He didn't know the man, or rather the boy he once was. All he saw was the man's failures—the shack, the dilapidated and unfinished house built of others' garbage, a wife who lost all of her teeth because they had such poor nutrition and hygiene, an alcoholic son who was also a thief and a criminal. He saw the outside of the man. He didn't know—as so many sons don't—who his father really was.

He also didn't see what strangers saw. At one point, Mac was a bus driver. On a route one day, he saw a rat caught in a gutter and struggling. Unable to witness any animal suffer, Mac stopped the bus full of passengers and went and released the rat and let it go on its way. He had a big heart.

He never raised his hands to his children, even when he wanted to shake them. And even when he wanted to beat the drunkenness and thievery out of his firstborn son, he resisted. He was not a violent man.

Dougie also didn't see what a consummate employee his father was. He worked for years as a security officer at a bank. He was so trustworthy; his employers gave him all the checks for delivery to other branch banks for the day. If there was a job to do, they knew Mac McCombs could be counted on to do it.

Mac McCombs never became a rich man. Though he loved to cook and spoke of one day owning his restaurant—he would have called it Mac's—he never got to do that, either. He did finish the home that still stands, a modest, two-story, modified Cape Cod/colonial hybrid, but everything else in life was hard going. After the kids grew up and moved out, he did enjoy some freedom and peace. He joined the Scottish Rite Masonic Temple. He found comradery among other men. After his Catholic wife left him, he became bitter against Catholics. He hated them with a fervent passion, channeling all his anger toward his first wife into the religion she practiced. But over the years, his prejudices softened. *He* softened. He read books. He tried to enjoy what little was left to the life he had created.

Toward the end of his life he suffered from dementia. He had outbursts and was so uncontrollable, he was put in an asylum.

He would have been all alone when he died had it not been for his son, Dougie, who showed up in his final hours. *Dougie: His pride and joy*. His one success in life. Though he would never have been able to say it.

When Dougie arrived in his father's room, he found the man out of his mind. He was unaware of where he was or who he was with. Dougie was repulsed at what he saw. His father was unkempt, uncared for, and the stench was overwhelming. No one deserved such indignity at the end of their life. No one.

Dougie pushed past the revulsion and looked deeply in his father's eyes. At the moment of his father's passing, just before Mac's soul moved from one side of the invisible veil that separates the living from the dead, Dougie felt that his father saw him and knew he was there. And he was right. In a brief moment of clarity, through his gray-blue eyes, Mac looked up and saw, standing beside his bed, his son Dougie. *He had come. He was there.* All his life Mac had felt alone. His father had turned his back on him. His first wife had left him. He felt the weight of the world on his shoulders to provide for his wife and children day in and day out. It was a thankless, Sisyphean task, the raising of children. He never had a soft place to land. There was no one coming to save him. No one there to help him pick up the ruins of his life. But then, in the next second, he realized that wasn't true either. He had Dougie. Dougie had worked beside him. Dougie had brought home his hard-earned money. Dougie had made something of himself. *And Dougie was here.* He was here to say goodbye and watch him pass from this hard life to the next, where he hoped he would at once find eternal rest. Love is showing up and sticking by someone, his wife Gladys had often said. Dougie had done both.

Dougie looked into his father's eyes one last time. It was a look that would haunt him forever. Long after his father had passed, it would be the only and lasting image he would have of him— this man, this mystery, this person who had brought him into this world. A man he struggled to understand. A man he struggled to love. A man, an imperfect, all-too-human man, who had also been his father. *His father.* The only one he would ever have. His link to the past, his future. There was nothing left to be done. Nothing left to say but two small, powerful words: "Thank you."

13

Love Doesn't Die; It Just Expands

*D*ouglas was a child again. He was holding his father's hand as a ribbon of highway spread out for miles before him. Trees swayed overhead. He was grateful for their shade and the cooling breeze. The sun was high in the sky, and he was sweltering. It was late afternoon, and waves of steam rose up from the blacktop, blurring his vision. As he squinted upward to take a look at his father, he saw his smile first, then his benevolent gray eyes. Little Dougie raised his chubby arms up to be carried. He was tired. So tired. His body ached all over.

"Can you carry me?"

"Dougie! Oh, little Dougie, are you tired, *Dougie?*"

As Dougie reached his hands up toward his father's hands, suddenly he became his father, his hands now reaching down. The roles had somehow been reversed, though Douglas couldn't comprehend why or how. He was no longer on the highway in the blazing hot sun, but rather he was standing in a museum in Korea. As he was looking down, a small Korean boy—no older than he had been, standing on the highway with his father—reached out and grabbed Douglas's pointer and middle fingers. The little boy began pulling him along—from exhibit to exhibit. Douglas had no choice but to follow the small boy's lead. The two walked together for some time. The boy never let go of his hand. When

the boy's father came for him, the boy began to wail and cry out—
reaching back for Douglas.

He was overwhelmed with love for this strange little boy.
"Everything is going to be okay. It's all going to be okay," Douglas
reassured him as he bent down and kissed the boy on the forehead
and sent him back to his father. As if he were an angel, the boy
looked up at him, perfect understanding in his eyes, and then disappeared out of sight.

Douglas was deeply affected. An overwhelming feeling of joy
washed over him. He couldn't wait to tell Suzy. He turned around
in the exhibit hall and heard her calling for him, "Douglas!
Douglas! Douglas!"

Douglas was confused. *Why is someone calling me "Douglas?" I
go by "Dougie." Or do I? And why am I in Korea? Where is the boy?
Where is my father? Suzy? Where is Suzy?*

Again, he heard his name as if coming high from the heavens.
A light, a bright light flashed before him. It was blinding.

Suddenly, a shadow developed. A small figure was coming
into view, leaning over him, her shoulder bandaged, her arm in
a sling.

"Suzy? Is that you?" Douglas said as he tried to focus. The
bright light of the windows overwhelmed his eyes, so he raised his
hands to shield them. Doing so, he felt incredible amounts of pain.
He was sore all over.

"You're awake! Oh, thank God! You're awake," Suzy said,
bending down to kiss his cheek.

"Where am I?" Douglas asked creakily, his voice wavering.

"You're in the hospital. You passed out on the top of the stairs
and took us both down," she said, grabbing water and a straw and
bringing them to his lips. "Here, sip this. Take it slow. You've been
out for a while."

Douglas sipped the water through a straw and took her all

in—*Suzy was here. She had stood by him.* Then he took her whole body in and noticed the full extent of her injuries.

"Oh my goodness, are you okay?" he said, pulling the straw away.

"Yes, yes, yes," Suzy said, hushing him, not wanting to draw attention to herself. "I just broke my collarbone. I'll be okay. Well, with a few surgeries, I'll be okay."

"A few? Oh no, Suzy, I'm so sorry," Douglas said, beginning to cry.

"Now, now, don't get upset. You're seriously injured too. You've hit your head, and it was quite a blow. I was so worried . . . you wouldn't . . ." Suzy couldn't even finish the thought, remembering all the blood on the sidewalk and waiting for the ambulance to come for them. "And this is all my fault. If I hadn't brought up the adoption and walked out . . . none of this . . ."

"No! Don't do that; don't blame yourself. It's not your fault," Douglas reassured her. "I have been feeling faint lately. I didn't want to tell anyone about it. I didn't realize how bad it had gotten. I have low blood pressure, and I must have stood up too quickly."

"That's what the doctors said." Suzy nodded. "You're lucky to have survived that fall. They said you have a very thick skull," she said with a smile.

"No surprise there," Douglas said, his sense of humor still intact.

"You have to stay here for a few days, Douglas. Mark's already been by to see you, and he's making all the arrangements and filled out all the forms. I didn't even know how to fill out the forms for you. I didn't know *so* much," Suzy said, shaking her head, almost in tears.

"That's not your fault. I am glad Mark was able to help," Douglas said. "After this, in the future, I will make sure you and I are both taken care of and know what to do in case something like this ever happens again."

"Listen to me, going on and on. I shouldn't be saying anything about forms and insurance. You just woke up. Do you need anything? Are you in any pain?" Suzy said, smoothing out his blankets and trying her best to care for him with one arm.

"Just sore. My head hurts," Douglas said, reaching up to feel the bandages.

"I'm sure," she said.

"Are you in lots of pain?" Douglas asked Suzy.

"I am, but I am not going to take pain medication. It's better if I don't. I'll be fine."

"Oh, Suzy, I hate that I did this to you. I can't imagine causing you any pain. The last thing I ever wanted to do was hurt you, bring you down."

"You didn't! There is nothing to apologize for," Suzy said, now sitting back down to get some rest.

"I have so much I want to tell you. So much I needed to say to you," Douglas said. "I had a dream. I dreamed of my father. He was a good man. He did his best. All these years, I didn't think he loved me or paid attention to me, but something happened in my dream. I realized that all this time he was carrying me. He loved me enough to take me with him on the road when he worked. He loved me enough to build a house for me and my family, even if it took his entire life. He loved me even though he couldn't say it. *Love isn't in the words, Suzy. It isn't in the words*." Douglas found himself on the verge of tears.

Suzy stood up again and leaned over Douglas to gently kiss his forehead. Douglas reached up and held her face and gazed deeply into her brown eyes.

"Love is inside of you and me," Douglas went on. "It's inside everyone. *It's energy*. It lasts beyond all time. I could feel my father's love. I could feel his father's, and his father's, and his father's, and all the love spanning back through all the generations of time. I could feel it building and pulsing through me.

Gathering momentum and giving me courage. Love is *courage*. Love is extending your heart even though you know it could be broken. Even though you know it won't be reciprocated. Love is patient. It is kind. It is true. It bears all things. It endures beyond time and space. Love is the most powerful force in the universe, uniting all of us to everyone and everything. It's the absence of fear. It's the absence of jealousy, control, and manipulation. Love is a magnet. It pulls people toward each other that are of the same pure energy, same light. It's what pulled you and I together."

"Oh Douglas, that's beautiful," Suzy whispered and kissed him again.

"In my dream, a boy, a little Korean boy came to me and reached up and grabbed my hand. Only it wasn't just a dream. *It was a memory*. I was in a Korean museum a long time ago, and a little boy took my hand and led me through the exhibit. It was one of the happiest, purest moments of my life. I had always wanted children. I had always wanted to be a father. But Hope didn't want that, so I put that part of me away in a box and put it up on a shelf. I let those dreams die a long time ago so Hope could have hers. But in Korea, I felt, even if it was just a few moments, what it must be like to love a child so unconditionally, so joyfully, so wholly that you would walk through fire to protect them. I also felt what it was like to be loved, to be needed, to be accepted, for no other reason than the fact that I was *just me*. And I realized then that my love for him and his love for me—it was magnetic. It was energy. It didn't just last in that one moment; it will survive throughout all time. *It's out there,* that *love. It still exists as energy, as light—as love*. That boy came back to me in my dream for a reason—he came to remind me that I still have all that love in my heart to give. I can give it. *I am ready to give it*."

"What are you saying, Douglas?"

"I am saying I want to be a father too, Suzy," Douglas said. "I know I am older than you—nearly seventy—but I have a lot of years in me left to live. You're only fifty, and you have so much love in you to give. I know you would make a wonderful mother. I want to be there with you every step of the way, help you in every possible way, for as long as I can in any way I can—even after I am gone. We came together for a reason bigger than us.

"Blood and bones and skin don't make us who we are. *Love* makes us who we are. The love we share makes us who we are. The love we pass on makes us who we are. The love we give to others selflessly makes us who we are. I love you so much. I don't want to spend a moment without you. I want to watch your love grow outward too—see it expand into the love of a mother—and see it expand into future generations—Scottish or not! Speaking of ancestry, if it weren't my curiosity about it, I would never have met you. I would never have gone on this journey. I learned so much on this journey about myself from my ancestors. I learned about love, about courage—which are in some ways the same thing. Both require one to move beyond fear.

"My ancestor Thomas was moved beyond fear to protect his sons, his family, his legacy. My ancestor John Gordon's wife moved beyond fear and jealousy and possession, and raised a child that wasn't her own. She *loved* Timothy as her own. My ancestor Alexander Macomb endured unfathomable pain and loss—his beloved wife and mother of his children. Like me, he couldn't return to his home after his beloved's death, but he overcame his fears and eventually married and loved another. My ancestor John McCombs got over his own father's betrayal and forgave him. Over time he understood his father—just like I eventually came to understand mine. Timothy was just doing what he thought was best and what he was capable of at the time. And my grandfather Norm was so much like me—such a dreamer, so dedicated to his family, but he was heartbroken after his son died. He couldn't recover. He spent the entire rest of his life despondent and depressed—so much so he identified with that pain. It's all he had and it's all he lived. I don't want that for me. I don't want that for us. And I realize now, as much as it was important to learn these things and know these things, I have come to a realization: Our bloodlines don't define us. Our pasts don't define us, and they don't determine our destinies.

"We're more than our bloodlines. *We're love lines. Love is what flows down the generations. Love is what collects and gathers in force and momentum and strength. Love. And I love you, Suzy Hamilton.*"

"Oh, Douglas, but look at us. We're two broken—quite literally—two broken human beings. Do you think we can do it? Do you think we have enough love to pass along?"

"In the universe, things have to break down to be reborn. Nothing truly ever dies. Energy just transforms. It exists forever and ever. We had to break down to be rebuilt. Everything that brought us here together, happened for a reason. You and I happened for a reason. Every experience we have had up until this moment has gotten us where we are today, to the people we are today. Even the heartbreak, the loss, the grief and pain, all of it taught us how to love better. I loved Hope with all my heart. I gave her everything. That doesn't die; it just expands. It's still out there. I can access it and reach it anytime. And just because I loved one person doesn't mean I can't love another. Love doesn't depreciate. Loving one person doesn't mean you can't love another. True love doesn't work like that.

"Our grief doesn't equal love. The extent to which we mourn and suffer doesn't ever equal the amount of love between two people. True love exists beyond suffering. True love exists, in its purest form, when we recognize and have gratitude for each other. I am grateful for all that Hope taught me—the good and the bad. I am grateful for the life I created with her—the traveling, the houses, the parties, the business and career that all flourished with her at my side. Without all of that I would not be where I am today—good and bad. We don't have to be perfect to love each other. We don't have to have clean slates and unmarred pasts to be able to fully cherish each other. We just have to be present with each other, accept each other for who we each are and who we are becoming. I don't regret my past, but I am ready to move on. I am ready to live, truly live. I am ready to stand on the top of the stairs and reach out, even if it means falling to the bottom, because I'm willing to do anything just to be together," Douglas said.

"Oh, Douglas, I don't know what to say," Suzy said, crying.

"Say you'll stick with me. Say you'll let me be by your side. Say we'll go through the rest of this journey together. I don't know where it will take us. I don't know how long I have. Heck, no one ever does. But all I know is that if I am going to go on this journey of living the rest of my life, I want it to be with you."

"I want that too, Douglas, so much," Suzy said.

"So this isn't the end," Douglas said with a smile.

"No, it's not the end."

"Love never ends," Douglas said, kissing Suzy's hand.

Acknowledgments

Thank you to the Greenleaf team for making the publishing process painless.

Thank you to Mark Collard for his unrelenting personal and professional support over the past twenty-five years. I love you, Mark.

Thank you, Mary Curran Hackett. Without your collaboration and support, this book would not exist.

Suky! My life partner. Your love and support kept me going and rekindled my interest in writing this novel. You are my Reason to Be.

About the Author

Norman McCombs was born in Amherst, New York, in a home built by his immigrant father. He graduated from Amherst Central High School, where he met his late wife, Grace. Norman went on to earn an AASEE from ECTI, along with a BSME and an ScD from State University New York at Buffalo while serving in the New York Army National Guard.

Norman is a Fellow of the American Society of Mechanical Engineers, which honored him with the EDISON Medal, their highest patent award. He has received numerous other awards for technical achievement, including the National Medal of Technology and Innovation from President Obama for developing the portable oxygen concentrator credited with saving and extending the lives of millions with lung diseases. He has over two hundred patents worldwide, primarily for air separation technology used for a myriad of oxygen applications around the world.

Norman is also an officier commander of the Chaîne des Rôtisseurs, as well as a sculptor, classical guitarist, and an avid fan of opera and the fine arts in general.